SHORTWAVE:

Dexter Wansel

Shortwave:

Edited by Jake George (www.sagewordsservices.com)

Cover artwork by Jake George (www.sagewordsservices.com)

A Sage Words Services Book
www.sagewordsservices.com

ISBN-13: 978-0615565538

ISBN-10: 0615565530

DEDICATION

This book is dedicated to my wife whose proof reading during the creative process helped me immensely. I wish to also dedicate this book to all veterans and active military personnel. Especially the men and women I was honored to serve with during my years in the U.S Army.

Contents

PART ONE: THE ANGEL... 3

CHAPTER 1.. 3

Washington D.C.. 3

CHAPTER 2.. 10

Washington D.C.. 10

CHAPTER 3.. 20

Three hours earlier, Washington D.C...................... 20

CHAPTER 4.. 25

CHAPTER 5.. 33

CHAPTER 6.. 36

CHAPTER 7.. 41

Washington D.C. Nine Hours Earlier 41

CHAPTER 8.. 56

Philadelphia PA, Sunday 10 p.m. 56

The Caribbean 57

CHAPTER 9.. 61

U.S. Coast Guard Cutter: 61

CHAPTER 10.. 72

The Caribbean: 72

CHAPTER 11 93

CHAPTER 12 108

Coast Guard Cutter Harpoon 108

SHORTWAVE: PART TWO 120

CHAPTER 13 120

The Flight 120

CHAPTER 14 136

CHAPTER 15 154

CHAPTER 16 163

SHORTWAVE: PART THREE 170

CHAPTER 17 170

CYCLOPS. 170

CHAPTER 18 179

CHAPTER 19 192

It was incredible 192

CHAPTER 20 206

CHAPTER 21 213

Shortwave: Part Four 219

THE ANGEL AND THE DEVIL TOO! 219

CHAPTER 22 219

CHAPTER 23 233

CHAPTER 24 246

CHAPTER 25 254

CHAPTER 26 257

CHAPTER 27 270

ACKNOWLEDGMENTS

I wish to thank God for all God's Love. I wish to thank
my folks for their love. I wish to thank my wife and all
of our children including the grand ones. To my
brothers and sisters thanks for being there. And finally,
I wish to thank Jake George without whose editing,
this book would not be. And of course, for all of his
Sage Words.

Dexter

PART ONE: THE ANGEL

CHAPTER 1
Washington D.C.

Adrian Perez cursed his rotten luck. Of all the restaurants in Georgetown, he had to choose this one to bring the dark and lovely Lisa Alvarez for another one of their lover's retreats in what was a volatile affair. *Don't panic! Just don't panic.* If he could make his way to the men's room, surely his wife Beverly, who was standing by the maître d desk, wouldn't notice him. *Miera!* So many things seemed to be going wrong these days. Maybe this time... Ah, but no.

There she was now, staring directly at him with a look of what could only be described as hurt and utter shock on her face.

Knowing she believed him to be in New York City at this very moment co-chairing a U.N. sponsored conference of the Organization of American States. He would not be able to use his considerable Latin charm to talk his way out of what was most certainly a dangerous and difficult situation. What was she doing here? *Of course, now I remember,* as he tried to avert his attention elsewhere. It must be that women's group she's so fond of.

What do they call themselves now? Women for the Homeless, or something like that. Yes, that's it! Women For The Homeless. They help homeless people get housing and then take them out to some museum or fancy restaurant to reacquaint them with the virtues of a civilized society. How stupid! And how so very like her to do this him. His hatred began to smolder, ready to burst into flames. He could barely control his temper.

Lisa Alvarez looked at him with a coy expression, "Adrian, isn't that your American whore just about to leave?" Adrian looked up just in time to see Beverly exiting by the front door. "Don't you think it's time you introduced us, dear Adrian?" she said, smiling just a little too sweetly. She took his left hand and brought it to her lips just as Beverly walked by their window table. Lisa then began to lick her tongue across his knuckles.

"Jesus! Not now, Lisa." But before he could pull away, Beverly momentarily stopped by the window without looking in. And just as quickly, she walked away as if nothing had happened. Adrian knew she had seen them. Damn it. She had seen and again his hatred threatened to explode inside of him.

Something will have to be done about the situation. And it would have to be done soon. Too much was at stake now to allow one stupid bitch to jeopardize it all.

No not one, but two stupid bitches. Yes, that's right. Dos putas. Looking at Lisa and feeling somewhat amused as his anger subsided. It would all be taken care of soon enough.

A waiter arrived to take their order. Adrian relaxed and allowed himself to be pampered while he enjoyed an exquisite dinner. After all there wasn't much he could do about things right now, but the time would come and... So long *Putas*.

Afterwards he and Lisa left the restaurant and retrieved his rental car from the valet service. On the drive back to the apartment, he kept secreted away in Germantown for clandestine meetings and such purposes as might arise, Adrian Perez took stock of himself. He was now forty-two years of age. In the past fifteen years since he had come to America as a young and dedicated courier for Castro and the Cuban government, he had done very well for himself indeed. Rising through the diplomatic ranks to become the chief attaché of the Cuban Consul in D.C., he had made a fortune along the way. A fortune only he knew about and which had been attained only at great risk.

Early on, he had taken an American wife, of old world stock, and they had two children, John and Jennifer. Her name at the time had been Beverly Stokes, one of her ancestors had come over on the Mayflower. For him it had certainly been a marriage of convenience. Having an American wife with good social ties had helped him to further his career along. And he thought in a prejudiced way that with his good white Cuban looks, (He was not one of those *mestizo* mongrels descended from African and *Taino* he so much hated) it had been relatively easy to win her over. Even today at 5'10" and 170 pounds, people often told him he looked like a young Omar Sharif. He liked Omar Sharif a lot. Had even once met him during a reception at the Egyptian Embassy.

Yes, he could be proud of his achievements. He had worked hard to get where he was. As he looked over at Lisa who rode quietly beside him, he could not help but think, here was another one of his achievements. As he ran his hand along her thigh, *How very beautiful this woman is.* But not only was she beautiful as he well knew, but also deadly. Her cover as the ambassador's assistant secretary was just that. But in reality she was a dangerous intelligence agent, and sadistic interrogator, handpicked by Castro himself! In time he had even attained her. *Mi dios*, life was wonderful.

She smiled at him. "Don't you think you should watch where you're going?" she said.

"Yes of course," he said but continued to rub his hand along her leg. "Lisa, I was just thinking. How about if we call it off for tonight. After what happened at the restaurant, it might be prudent for me to go home and smooth things over with Beverly. After all, we don't want to jeopardize everything, now that were so close to having it all. Do we, dear?"

Lisa's reaction was swift and violent. She took Adrian's right hand off her leg and savagely twisted it counter clockwise at the wrist. He yelped in sudden pain and shock, but she did not let go. "If you think I'm going to continue to let you put me off think again, *estupido*." She hissed, twisting even harder.

"Okay, okay." He screamed again, and Lisa let go. He pulled the car over to the side of the road. "Why did you have to do that?" he cried, rubbing his wrist. "You could have broken it." *Jesus Christ, the bitch has gone too far this time. She will pay dearly for this outrage.*

Lisa looked at him and smiled. "Yes Adrian, I think you are right after all. You can take me home now."

Adrian put the car back in drive and pulled out into the street. Sweat was beginning to work its way down his neck as he fought to fight back the fear gorged in his throat. He felt somewhat embarrassed when he dropped Lisa off at her apartment.

As she got out the car she turned and said, "If you don't leave her Adrian, I will kill her and you will have to come to me." She shut the door and let herself into the apartment.

Stunned, he couldn't believe what had occurred tonight. He would have to move up his timetable a lot sooner than he planned. "*Puta.*" He spat, rubbing his wrist. *I'll make sure that when the time comes, my people take their time with her.* Still in thought, he sped away, too quickly, and barely missed running into another car. He slammed on the brakes and stopped. Closing his eyes and breathing deeply, he was able to collect himself. This time he pulled off at a normal rate of speed, and as he drove home his thoughts were as dark as the cold autumn night that surrounded him.

Beverly Perez closed the front door of her Georgian styled manor and put her coat in the hallway closet. She made her way to the kitchen and put a pot of coffee on the stove. It was a good thing that the kids were spending the weekend at their grandparents because she could not face anybody else after what happened tonight. Tomorrow the local gossips would be having a field day, and at some point she would have to make her children aware of what happened, before they were hurt by some off chance remark; or something worse.

She went upstairs to her bedroom and removed the clothes and shoes she had been wearing that day and put on a warm blue goose down robe with matching slippers. Returning to the kitchen she poured herself a cup of hot coffee. "How could this thing have happened," she whispered to herself as she sat at the breakfast table. For some time now she had known that her husband was not the man she once believed he was.

She even had suspected him of having an affair some time ago, but to have seen it for herself had been more than she could take. Her world was coming apart around her, and there was nothing she could do about it.

She put her arms around herself and began to sob in uncontrollable waves. She didn't know how long she had been sitting there crying, but when she looked up Adrian was standing there.

He just stood there and looked at her.

"Well," she said, "aren't you going to say anything?" She wiped the tears from her eyes.

He smiled at her and said, "But my dear what is there to say? Aren't you happy here in your beautiful home with your beautiful children? And aren't those tears of happiness you are crying? Well, aren't they?" he insisted, but this time without a smile. "Because if they aren't you can leave at any time you are ready."

He shifted closer to her with a look of menace shadowing his face.

Fear surged through her, and she bowed her head.

"No, I didn't think so," he said. And he turned and walked out of the kitchen without another word.

Beverly Perez got up and stood wavering. She had to hold on to the table to keep herself from falling. Somehow she made her way to the living room where she laid down on the couch and cried herself to sleep. She had disturbing dreams that night.

Dreams of unseen events that caused her to turn restlessly. Dreams of something evil. Dreams of death and destruction.

CHAPTER 2

Washington D.C.

Jennifer Perez liked walking home from school on Fridays the most. There was something exhilarating about being able to forget about homework and just talking with friends as they walked along. On this Friday though, she, her mother, and brother would be preparing to take a train in the morning. All the way to British Columbia, Canada to visit their aunt Beatrice. She had never been outside of D.C. and had a million questions to ask her mother when she got home. Her brother John had told her that Canada was full of grizzly bears, and she wasn't sure if she should believe him or not. The trip would be so much fun. She was so excited she hurried home without talking to anyone.

When she got home she found the house deserted, so she put her books down, and got some milk out of the frig. She wanted some corn chips, too, when she heard a noise that sounded like shouting coming from her parents' bedroom. She walked up the steps to the bedroom where she found her mother and father standing face to face in the midst of a heated argument. They did not see her come in.

Her father was saying, "I will not allow you to do this, I tell you. You have no right."

Her mother replied, "Adrian, there is nothing else to say. You have two weeks."

Jennifer's father stood there for a moment and then like lightning, he struck her mother across the face with the back of his hand. Jennifer's mother fell hard against the dresser, and then to the floor, where he began to kick her repeatedly. Jennifer screamed and ran to her mother's side. She put her arms around her pleading for him to stop. But he would not.

Now it was Jennifer who was receiving the brunt of his attack. The pain from his kicks was so bad she thought she would pass out. Beverly was finally able to get up, and charged him with her head down butting him in the stomach, knocking the wind out of him.

With a loud whoosh Adrian doubled up in pain and fell to his knees. Beverly grabbed her car keys from the dresser and helped Jennifer get to her feet. They ran out of the bedroom, down the stairs, and out of the house. When they took a moment to look at each other they saw only suffered minor bruises. Though Beverly had a swelling under her right eye.

They got in her car and Beverly drove off down the street, where she hailed the first police cruiser they saw. Upon telling the officer what had happened, he decided to follow them back to the house and talk to Adrian. But Adrian was gone.

Just then her brother John arrived home from school and her mom asked the officer if he would remain at the house until they could get their bags, packed the previous night, out of the house and into the car. Beverly explained about their trip in the morning and he agreed to wait. He also made out a domestic violence report which he had her sign in case she decided to press charges.

After the bags had been stowed away, Beverly checked to see that all the tickets and travelers checks were in her handbag. Having assured herself that everything was in order she locked the house, and then thanked the officer and started on her journey. They were thankful when he decided to follow them to the beltway, where with a wave of his hand, he finally turned off in another direction.

Beverly drove to a motel she knew of near Dulles airport while she struggled to maintain her composure. She constantly looked into the rear view mirror afraid that Adrian could be following them. She also saw that her face was swelling and a black bruise had developed under her right eye. *Thank God Jennifer wasn't seriously hurt.*

The Bastard! The goddamn Bastard! Assaulting his own child for Christ sakes! She knew then she really hadn't known him at all.

She pulled into the motel and angrily leaped from the car before renting adjoining rooms for herself and her children. Once inside, she decided to explain to her children everything that had transpired before and over the past two weeks. She wanted to make sure there could be no doubt in their minds how serious a situation they were really in with their father. Though she wasn't sure how they would respond. John had become sullen and withdrawn when he found out about the attack. He had also voiced an opinion that maybe what happened to them wasn't her and Jennifer's fault. And for a twelve year old boy, it was a sad revelation. The father he thought he knew and loved may have really been a beast.

Nonetheless she proceeded to tell them the facts. She met their father when she was working for the Cuban Consul as a secretary for an assistant director named Hector Gomez, a Cuban National. He introduced them one night after work.

Adrian was very handsome and charming. She immediately fell in love with him and after a whirlwind romance which lasted six months, they were quietly married. John was born a few months later. But soon after, things began to change. Oh he was always the provider and made sure that her needs were taken care of, but he also became more distant. After Jennifer was born he began to stay away for days and weeks at a time, saying that he was on important assignments for his country.

To quell her fears he moved her and the children into a stately manor in Chevy Chase, Maryland. Far too expensive for a Cuban diplomat, but she never questioned where he got money to afford such a well to do life style. She always justified her own motives by saying her children deserved the best. When in reality, she was afraid he might leave her penniless and destitute if she asked too many questions.

At that point, she broke out in tears, while Jennifer tried to mollify her. She took a moment to regain her composure and then continued. She knew now how wrong she had been. The price of being married to him was way too high because now their lives were in jeopardy.

John jumped up off the bed and shouted, "What do you mean? Does Dad want to kill us now? What have you done?"

Beverly told him to sit down and she would try to explain. John sat down even more sullen than before. She knew they were young, but they had to know the truth. Beverly told them that a couple of weeks ago after seeing their father with another woman, she decided she had enough.

She called her friend Winona Rhoads, one of the women in her club, whose husband was a private detective, and asked for his help. She wanted to get proof of Adrian's infidelities before she sought a divorce. Then and only then she believed, would he co-operate and agree to a fair settlement.

She talked to Mr. Rhoads and after a few questions about Adrian; he agreed to help and said he would call her in about a week. When he finally did call, he explained that he needed to see her that very night and it was a matter of great importance.

She met the detective at the Chevy Chase shopping mall in Hillary's ice cream shop.

He was already there, sitting at a table eating frozen yogurt when she arrived. She sat down across from him. Without a word he handed her a large manila envelope. Nervously, she thumbed through the documents and pictures she found inside. The pictures proved that Adrian was cheating on her all right and for some reason she breathed a sigh of relief.

The other documents were a mystery to her, and she inquired as to what they were. The detective finished eating his yogurt and wiped his mouth before answering. "First of all," he said, "let me say that this was the easiest job I ever had to do and certainly the most gratifying. I mean this guy; your husband is a real piece of work. Let me tell you. I wouldn't even dream of charging you for this." He took a notebook from his pocket and proceeded to read from it.

"The day after I talked to you, I caught up with the bastard at the Cuban Consul where you said he would be and followed him to an apartment in Georgetown leased in the name of one Hector Gomez."

Beverly dropped her napkin in surprise. "I used to work for him."

"I know," said Rhoads, and continued. "That night and on subsequent nights he had numerous visitors who would stay until about midnight. At which point he would return to your house here in Chevy Chase as you well know."

She understood because Adrian always came home late.

"During these nights I was able to take the pictures you see before you with some very sophisticated equipment and also to gain entrance into the apartment long after your husband and his friends had left. These are your copies by the way. I've got the negatives stored away in a very safe place, because we will need them very soon.

"That apartment is decked out like a real swinger's showplace as the pictures show, but what I found to be most interesting was the wall safe behind one of the velvet nudie pictures on the bedroom wall. I haven't seen safe like it in years. It's an old Wells Fargo model and would you believe, was wide open when I found it," he insisted with an innocent look on his face that made Beverly smile.

"So I said what the heck and took pictures of everything inside that safe before locking it back up the

15

way I found it. Oops! I didn't say that," he said. And they both had a good laugh. After a few moments Bill Rhoads became serious. "Mrs. Perez, I believe we're sitting on a time bomb here. These documents are classified and are the property of the N.S.A. They seem to reveal in detail U.S. covert activities in Cuba. And if that's the case, then your husband is up to his neck in some deep shit. If you will excuse my French.

"I've already made a few calls to some friends of mine at the N.S.A., and expect to hear back from them tomorrow about the authenticity of these papers. But I have no doubt." Looking directly into her eyes, he said without blinking, "Ma'am I think your husband's a spy."

Beverly thought for a moment and knew he was right. She didn't know how she knew, she just did. "Now I know you need time to get your affairs in order, but I think you will agree that it's our duty to do something about this."

"Yes. Of course. I know you're right," she said.

"Will a few weeks be enough Mrs. Perez?"

He seemed to know what was the right thing to do, so she said, "Yes. Three weeks. That will be fine. I trust your judgment."

He got up from the table and extended his hand which she took. "Sometimes people can be just plain mean Mrs. Perez. I'm sorry your husband had to turn out that way."

Beverly said, "So am I Mr. Rhoads, so am I."

John and Jennifer looked at each other. Beverly had finished telling the children what she knew about their father.

"Well, that's it then," John said.

"No... Not quite," answered Beverly. "This past week since I've been putting our trip together, I haven't spoken to your father until today."

"Did you tell him about, about the spy stuff and all?" Jennifer asked.

"Yes. I confronted him with it. Though he denied everything, I told him he had two weeks to leave the country and go back to Cuba before the authorities came for him."

"What did Dad say?" John asked with tears in his eyes.

"He said they couldn't touch him because of his diplomatic immunity. But when I reminded him that in cases of espionage, diplomatic immunity was almost always revoked, he became enraged."

"That's when he started hitting you? Right Mommy?" insisted Jennifer.

"Yes that's right honey. I want to thank you for what you did back there at the house. That was very brave and I'm proud of you."

"Oh, that's all right." Jennifer said.

Beverly slowly rose up from the bed, exhausted from the revelations she had shared with her children. "I think it's time we went and found someplace to eat." They left their room and went to the restaurant that was directly across the street. Beverly told them they could have anything they wanted.

But nonetheless they all ate in solitude.

Upon returning to the motel room, John and Jennifer propped themselves in front of the TV in the one room, while Beverly called Winona Rhoads from the other. The phone rang a few times before a woman answered. Beverly said, "Hello, is Winona there?"

"I'm sorry," the voice said, "but she is unable to come to the phone right now. May I ask whose calling?"

"It's Beverly Perez, and I was just calling to speak to Winona. Might I ask whom I'm talking to?" she asked a little worried.

"This is Winona's mother, and I guess you haven't heard yet."

"Heard what yet?" Beverly asked feeling nausea clutch at her stomach.

"Winona's husband, Bill was killed earlier this evening in a car accident."

"Oh my God," she said as wave after wave of nausea hit her like a sledge hammer. She became too dizzy to hold the phone in her hand, and it fell to the floor.

Beverly sat on the edge of the bed in agonizing distress. She laid back and closed her eyes. She cried hard then, she tried to believe it wasn't her fault. But the guilt wouldn't go away. *Why? Why? Why?* she thought. *Why?*

Night had fallen by the time Beverly was able to sit up again. She wiped the wetness from her face wincing in pain at the tenderness of her swollen eye. She got up and walked to the window. Outside planes were taking off from Dulles into the night sky.

The stars were out and it seemed so peaceful. But she knew Adrian was out there watching and waiting. He would have no mercy for her or her children when he finally caught up with them. As she watched the planes taking off, suddenly she had an idea. Adrian and his people would more than likely be waiting for them at Union Station. After all he was a spy and she knew he probably had people watching her now.

"What if..." She reached for the phone.

CHAPTER 3

Three hours earlier, Washington D.C.

In another part of town, Winona's husband, Bill Rhoads, had just locked up his office and was getting ready to go home. As he walked into the street to the driver's side of his car he didn't notice a dark blue SUV pull off from the sidewalk about a block away and head in his direction.

While he fumbled with the remote for his car, the dark blue SUV picked up speed. When he finally managed to get the door open, the SUV was bearing down upon him at about 60 miles per hour. He barely had enough time to turn and see the SUV coming, when it struck him head on, tearing the door off his car at the same time. For a moment he found himself on the hood of the car. But whoever was driving slammed on the brakes, screeching to a halt.

His body was flung into the air and hit the ground where he bounced a few yards. The pain in his back was excruciating. His chest had been crushed during the impact and he suffered severe internal injuries, but he knew none of this. All he felt was pain. As he lay on his side, he could see the tires of little blue sedan about ten feet away.

Incredibly, he heard the vehicle's engine revving up again and saw the tires surge towards him. The SUV ran over him, this time catching his body underneath, and dragging him about fifty feet before finally speeding off. Leaving his body behind in the street; an almost unrecognizable mass of torn flesh and broken bones. Bill Rhoads was already dead before any passerby could stop and help. A number of people saw what happened, but later on, after the police arrived on the scene, only a few could give a good description of the fleeing vehicle. And no one could remember the number of the license plate.

The driver parked the blue SUV just a few blocks away. He exited the car and walked to the metro where he caught the blue line to Bethesda. He slipped out of the doors unnoticed and went up the long escalator to the street. Parked nearby was a white BMW, which he slid into and started up. Inside was a cellular phone. He picked it up punched in a number and said, "'This is Shortwave 3. There is no static. I repeat, there is no static" He hung up and pulled the car quickly onto the street. He still had a train to catch.

Autumn had come early and there was coldness in the air as Beverly and the kids waited for the shuttle bus to take them from the self-service parking lot to the front entrance of Dulles International Airport.

They had all donned coats before checking out of the motel. But some of the coldness they felt was fear, that hung over them like a shroud, as they made their way from the motel to the airport.

Even John, after learning about the death of Mr. Rhoads, couldn't help but feel it, too. When the shuttle bus arrived they clambered aboard with their luggage. They had their choice of seats. Only two other people were on board the bus.

When they reached the airport entrance, Beverly checked around first by looking out the windows of the bus to make sure they weren't being followed. She felt reasonably sure that they hadn't been. With luggage in hand, they exited the bus and entered the airport. Trying hard to look like a family going on vacation and to attract no undue attention.

Dulles International was a flurry of activity as weekend travelers hurried to catch their flights or queued up to purchase tickets at various airline booths. Beverly had the kids stand in the line for Eastern while she went to the pay phone. She dialed her home number and it rang twice before somebody picked it up. She listened, waiting for the person to say something. When no one did she hung up, shaking all over. She took her phone book out of her handbag and looked up another number, which she dialed. After getting an answer she talked for a few minutes then said goodbye.

She walked back to the kids who had almost reached the counter and took out her Master Card. When it was their turn to be waited on, she told the woman that she had called earlier and made reservations on the 9:30 flight to Orlando. The woman checked her computer and said yes, they were confirmed on that flight and would have to hurry if they were going to make it. As soon as they checked their baggage and received their tickets and boarding passes they walked quickly towards their Eastern gate number.

But hearing the final boarding call for their flight over the PA system, they began to run. Thankfully the airport was not busy and they rushed through the metal detectors and ran to the gate just as the attendant was closing the outer tunnel door.

"Wait! Wait." Beverly shouted and the attendant waved them through as he took their tickets. They ran through the tunnel and onto the plane. A stewardess closed the plane's door behind them. Once in their seats, Beverly was able to relax. They were safe for the moment.

As the plane began to roll back she looked out her window and in the waiting area she saw a man standing there looking out the window at the plane. Her heart leaped into her throat and a cold sweat came over her until she heard someone behind her say, "Oh look honey there's Daddy. Wave bye bye. He will be on the next flight to join us." In a moment the man at the window smiled as he began to wave. Beverly lay back in her seat and struggled to fight back the tears as the plane taxied out to the runway.

She looked at Jennifer and John who were reading magazines they had found in the seat bins in front of them. They understood the journey ahead. During the next few weeks they must go into hiding. Their lives depended upon it. The authorities would soon know the truth about Adrian after her phone call at the airport had seen to that. But until they caught up with him or he went back to Cuba they would have to keep running. In her heart she knew the chase had only just begun.

Dexter Wansel

CHAPTER 4

Adrian Perez was daydreaming thinking back, on the twisted paths his life took, as he waited in his car. He was only five years old in 1955 when his father left Cuba for Mexico with Fidel Castro to prepare for the overthrow of Fulgencio Batista and his government. When they returned in 1956. Castro and his followers were almost annihilated in their first attack.

Being sought after by government troops, Castro moved what was left of his group, along with their families, to the Sierra Maestra where they waged a guerrilla campaign until January 1 1959. On that day the *Fidelistas* took control of the country. Surprisingly they numbered fewer than a thousand. They called themselves The 26th of July Movement. After Castro's ill-fated attack on the *Moncada* military fortress in Santiago on July 26 1953.

As a group, they had only vague political plans, hardly any support and no governing skills. Nonetheless they attracted a following from among the peasants, the workers, the young and idealistic. Adrian was not among these. He was nine years old by then and had seen his father become a hero of the revolution and a member of the *Partido Communista de Cuba*. The Communist Party, only to live a peasant's lifestyle while Castro and his top henchmen lived like royalty.

The years of hunger and hardship in the mountains, where he also saw his mother die, instilled in him a hidden desire for money and material wealth.

When the new regime abolished capitalism between 1959 and 1963 it left a smoldering, anger in the boy. By the time he was a university student his hatred of Castro and his policies was to influence him in everything he did; though he never allowed himself to reveal his thoughts to anyone.

He knew Castro did not tolerate discontent and any exposure could mean imprisonment and even death. Even for the son of a hero the revolution.

It was during his later years as a university student that he first met Hector Gomez. Gomez was a professor of western culture and politics and Adrian believed this man could help him. Without too much trouble he achieved highest honors in the professor's class. Gomez was duly impressed with his bright and gifted student, and soon the two men formed a friendship that was to become invaluable to the younger man.

When Gomez was chosen by Castro to become assistant Director of the Cuban Consul in Washington D.C., he immediately picked Adrian to accompany him as a junior attaché. At last Adrian would be able to realize his dream.

A few days before they left, Gomez was to receive orders from Castro and unwittingly help Adrian attain his goals in the process.

During his stay in the U.S. Gomez was directed to receive covert payments in American dollars from various drug traffickers who wanted to use Cuban soil in the form of airstrips or bases of operation in order to expand their drug trade. Adrian immediately seized upon this directive as his chance to cast off the chains of mediocrity and talked a reluctant Gomez into allowing him to be the pickup man. After all there was no betraying Castro.

In his very first week in the U.S. Adrian was able to put his plans to the test.

His first clandestine meeting was with a Columbian pilot who had more than 50 million dollars for the Castro regime.

In what was to be a bold and daring move. Adrian informed this man that the price had gone up by ten percent. The pilot who became indignant and very angry threatened not to pay the increase. Adrian simply told him he could take it up with Castro if he wished to and the pilot, after some thought, acquiesced without calling Adrian's bluff.

Once the word got around to all the other traffickers in the U.S., it became a matter of routine for Adrian or one of his subordinates to show up at a chosen place at the appointed time.

Then the transaction of specified sums of money which Adrian funneled back to Cuba through a network of offshore accounts of his own design, less ten percent was made. His one daring move had been a stroke of genius. In the fifteen years since the first transaction, no one had caught on to his embezzlement and in that time his secret Swiss bank account had grown to over 50 million dollars. Only on a few occasions had he found it necessary to cover his tracks. And for this purpose he masterminded a secret network of people who worked for him and him alone.

Numbering twelve in size. Five of which were professional killers, (he called them pest control) and the other employees at various U.S. Government agencies. He called his organization "Shortwave" in honor of his father who had been a shortwave radio operator during the revolution. His people in the government would acquire classified documents which he used to his own glorification in the eyes of the Castro regime.

And pest control would take out anyone who threatened the organization, or got too close to his money. He had made himself invaluable to Castro, and he intended to keep it that way as long as possible. Periodically in matters of the greatest secrecy, he would fly back to Cuba and meet with Castro himself.

Those times were indeed momentous. He would talk to the great man at length on any number of subjects and then with Lisa, (who always escorted him on these trips) he would bask away in the warm sunshine on the beautiful beaches of the *Jardines de la Reina*, (Queen's Gardens), where Castro kept one of his villas for entertaining his most trusted and loyal followers. On these occasions, Fidel Castro always loved to talk about the old days when he and Earnesto (Che) Guevara, along with Adrian's father and others, shocked the world with their revolution.

Sometimes he lectured Adrian not to become enamored with the riches America had to offer. "Because one day," he insisted, "you will return home to your rightful place among the people."

At these times Adrian was cautious not to reveal the revulsion he felt for the man. At the very least he knew he would never return to Cuba and the glorified revolution that had in fact become nothing more than bitter enslavement and poverty for the people. With the help of his organization and a good plastic surgeon, he would take on a new identity, and the man the world knew as Adrian Perez would be no more.

Yes, he was cautious about what he said and did around Castro. The man was a fox. One small slip on his part and Castro would surely smell his deception. He was always relieved to return to the U.S. after one of his Cuban trips. In the U.S. he felt safe and in control of his own destiny, a destiny that certainly had its dangers, but likewise its benefits.

Adrian realized he'd been daydreaming and went back to watching the street.

When Beverly had knocked the wind out of him, he had gotten up and sought to follow her and Jennifer outside. But when he got there they were already gone. He got into his own car and drove down the street a couple of blocks where he pulled over and parked. As he sat and waited he got a call on his cell phone.

He picked it up and listened and then hung up with a smile. *Well that's that!*

They had to come back for the clothes. And when they did, he would follow them to make sure they went to the train station. Somewhere he knew, from the call he had just received.

Shortwave 3 would be waiting for them. The call had revealed something else too. The man that was following him the previous week would follow him no more. His organization had learned he was a private eye named Bill Rhoads. Though they still hadn't found out who he was working for, they did discover where his office was and set him up to be taken out there. That he was dead, there could be no doubt.

Shortwave 3 was the best and most efficient operative in pest control. Never had he failed to finish a job that he started. *The man was simply frightening.* He thought for a moment that maybe he should feel sorry for Beverly and the kids. After all they were his family. But the pain he still felt in his stomach from Beverly's head butt reminded him how much of a threat she had become and quickly dissolved any husbandly or paternal feelings he still might have nurtured towards them.

At that moment Beverly and Jennifer drove by followed by a police cruiser. *Damn!* He couldn't take the chance of following them now and being seen. A problem with the police could very well upset the wheels he had already put in motion.

As soon as they were far enough away he turned his car around and headed towards the consul where he still had some unfinished business to tend to. Lisa Alvarez was waiting for him when he got there. After he signed in with security he went to his office where he found her sitting on the large chaise sofa he kept in the outer room.

She said, "*Ola* Adrian."

"Hello," he replied.

"Why do you continue to avoid me, *mi amour*?" Lisa said pouting. "You're not still are upset with me because of that night in the car are you?" she asked getting up, walking over to him and putting her arms around his waist. "You know I never meant to hurt you."

"Yes Lisa. I know," he replied. "It's just that... well... I've been busy with the Russians as you know," he said, regarding an ongoing conference between the

Cubans and the Russians concerning trades of which he was a senior negotiator.

"I just haven't had the time to see you that's all," he insisted.

Lisa said, "Oh you and your boring meetings. But I must see you Adrian." Then she said threateningly, "And I will see you tonight! And no more fooling around. I'm tired of waiting! Do you understand? Do you?"

Adrian looked at her and smiled his best Omar Sharif smile and said, "Yes darling. I understand. No more fooling around."

Lisa looked at him a little doubtful and said, "Do not play with me Adrian. You must mean it this time."

"I do mean it Lisa," he said. "After tonight I will be yours and yours only."

Lisa looked in his eyes a moment then threw her arms around his neck and kissed him fervently on the lips. "Oh Adrian you will never regret this. I will make you forget that you ever had to marry that woman in the first place."

"I know you will," Adrian said as he pulled her arms down. "But there are a few things I must do first like get some things from the house! If it's okay. I will meet you tonight at the apartment. Say around 9 p.m.?"

"Yes of course," Lisa said as she picked up her things and walked to the door of the office.

Before she left she turned to Adrian and said, "I will use my key and have a good Cubano supper waiting for you when you get there.

"And the dessert will be even better my darling." she said with a demure look in her eyes. She turned and left.

Adrian stood there for a while then walked over to his desk. He picked up the phone and made a call. He talked to someone about ridding his apartment of bugs and told them it would be fine if they were able to do it tonight around 8:30. After thanking them he hung up. It was time he knew to put his final plan in motion. He called Hector Gomez and talked for a few minutes. Afterwards he stood up from the desk and looked around his office without taking anything, he walked to the door, locked it, and after signing out with security, he left the Cuban consul for the very last time.

CHAPTER 5

Lisa Alvarez was taking a shower in the bath adjoining the bedroom of Adrian's apartment. She could smell the lamb she had left cooking in the stove in the kitchen and knew it was almost done. She had cooked the rice and beans earlier and all that was left to do was make the salad. When Adrian got there they would eat and spend their first night of the rest of their lives happily together.

As she turned off the water in the shower she was about to get out when she noticed a large shape just outside the plastic shower curtain. Her heart skipped a beat, she cried, "Adrian, you *chinga*! Don't scare me like that." Angrily she drew back the curtain. In front of her stood two men she had never seen before. One of them had a handgun with a silencer attached to it, and the other held a length of thin rope.

"*Oh Mi Dio*!" Lisa said softly. "Please! Where is Adrian?" she asked trying to cover herself with a towel. She knew she would get no answer. She also knew then that Adrian was not going to be there.

And in a sudden rage she kicked at the man holding the gun, catching him off guard and nearly knocking the gun out of his hand. Surprised, he grunted in pain and stepped forward striking her on top of the head with the barrel of the gun.

She crumpled unconscious, out of the tub, onto the bathroom floor where the two men lifted her up and moved her into the bedroom. They unrolled a large piece of plastic and laid her on it. And when she came to, she found herself gagged and laying on the bedroom floor. Her feet had been lashed together and her hands were tied behind her back. She watched as the one of the men who had left the room came back wearing clear plastic gloves and carrying the same carving knife she had used to cut up the lamb for Adrian's dinner She had done the same thing as part of her job and enjoyed inflicting pain. She shuddered, knowing that now she would be on the receiving end and prayed for unconsciousness.

He stood over her and said, "Adrian sends his regards and says to tell you he won't be able to be here for supper tonight. So he asked us to keep you entertained instead."

With that he kneeled down beside her and began to slowly push the knife in her body just below the rib cage and then pulled it out. Blood poured down her side as she tried to scream.

He kept finding new places to push the knife in. It was not until late in the evening that Lisa finally passed out and subsequently died from her many stab wounds.

The two men wrapped her body up in the plastic, along with her clothes and belongings and covered it with one of the blankets from the bed. They took the body out the back door under the cover of darkness and placed it in the trunk of a car they had parked there.

After making sure that everything was clean inside the apartment, they got in the car and drove outside the city to an abandoned warehouse. Where they removed the body from the car and dumped it inside an old building, then drove back to the city and parked the car on a street picked at random.

Since the car was stolen it really didn't matter. They got out and walked away into the night.

Adrian was waiting in his car when he got the call and afterwards he went back to the apartment. First checking to see there were no telltale traces left lying around. He then took out a bottle of his best wine and sat down to a delicious supper of Cuban style lamb with rice and beans. He toasted pest control on a job well done and finishing his meal, went to bed and had a good night's sleep.

CHAPTER 6

The next afternoon Shortwave 3 stood on Amtrak platform number six at Boston station waiting for the Canadian Express which had left Washington D.C. earlier that Saturday morning. He had driven all night to reach Boston in time to catch this train. He made note that the weather was much colder this far north and reflected on why he had driven so far.

He decided not to take a chance boarding the train in Washington, where he was known and someone might recall seeing or recognizing him. When the train finally arrived he took a seat in the cafe car and ordered a diet Pepsi.

Looking out the window he thought that it could be a hard winter that year. When the train began to move out of the station, he casually got up and walked back to the sleeping car section until he found his sleeper number. Upon entering the tiny room he locked the door behind him.

He didn't have much time; the next stop was only five minutes away in a small village called Milltown, where the train would pick up additional freight cars carrying vehicles for transport to Canada.

He opened up the luggage bag he was carrying. Inside the bag was H2, a plastic explosive and a time controlled detonating device.

He set the timer for 6 p.m., three hours away, closed the bag and stored it in a compartment beneath the seat. He then left the room and locked the door behind him. As he walked by the sleeper next to his, he thought about the three people inside and wondered if they possibly could have seen him. But how could they?

And even if they did, they wouldn't recognize him. Adrian had always thought it prudent not to mix business with family. *A smart man that Adrian.* Shortwave 3 returned to the cafe car and this time had a vodka and tonic. As soon as the train reached Milltown he disembarked and waved to the driver of the car waiting for him. He got in and they drove back to Boston where he said goodbye, picked up his own car, and started the long drive back to D.C.

Three hours later, Amtrak Canadian Express train 101 bound for British Columbia was slowly crossing the mile long Waterford International Bridge connecting the U.S. with Canada, when a terrific explosion tore two sleeping cars from the tracks and over the bridge dragging both ends of the train down into the gorge 1200 feet below.

All 232 people on board were either killed, or would die before anyone could reach them in the coming night. On the drive back to D.C., Shortwave S3 heard the news about the explosion on the radio. He was mildly surprised to hear that the entire train had been destroyed by the explosion and the resulting crash. He merely considered it good luck on his part.

It would be impossible now for the authorities to put all the pieces together. All in all it was a job well done he thought and perversely congratulated himself.

Picking up the cell phone he made the call to Adrian and said, "'This is Shortwave 3 at station number two. There is no static I repeat, there is no static. Over." He hung up and continued his drive back to Washington D.C. But this time he was wrong.

Shortwave 3 hadn't needed to make the code call. Adrian had already seen what happened. While he sat waiting in his apartment with the TV on, every single station in town had been interrupted with news bulletins of the train wreck. Helicopters were beaming live pictures of the wreckage across the country. Maybe even the world.

And Adrian was appalled at the carnage. He sat there numb with the realization of what had happened. Shortwave 3 was only supposed to take out the one car, the one with his wife and the kids on it.

He had gone through Beverly's pocketbook the day before yesterday and seen the tickets with the sleeper number. He passed the information along to Shortwave 3, with specific orders on how he wanted the job done. But something must have gone wrong. And now all hell was breaking loose.

It would be only a matter of hours before the press came looking for him. Some smart D.C. reporter would check reservations on this end and put two and two together. He had to get back to the house where he could play the role of the aggrieved husband and father for a few days... Until his final preparations were complete. Then Adrian Perez would be no more. When Shortwave 3's call came in, Adrian had already left the apartment.

That same night, a detective, Todd Morrison, sat in the living room of his former partner's house, consoling his wife. Bill Rhoads had been his partner on the police force. A veteran of twenty years before he had retired the previous year and gone into private practice. When Bill had been killed the day before, he had immediately rushed to the house to be by Winona Rhoads' side as a friend.

But tonight when Winona had called him and asked him to come over because she had some news about her husband's death, he was there as a detective.

When she was able to, Winona told him that the night before; she had received a call from an acquaintance of hers who had hired Bill to do a job. But due to her state of mind she did not realized the importance of the call until now. The woman, she said had told her that Bill may have been killed for trying to help her.

Winona said, "At first I thought she meant Bill's accident had occurred while he was doing something for her. But now I'm not so sure." Detective Morrison asked her for the woman's names but Winona said that was the funny thing about it. She could remember the woman's voice but not her name.

After some thought Detective Morrison asked if he could have the keys to Bill's office and his safe. And in the morning he would go through Bill's files and see what he could come up with. Winona gave him the keys and said, "It's a funny thing about that."

Morrison said, "What?"

"Wells it's just that when I heard her voice she sounded like she was in some kind of trouble."

Morrison commented. "If it has anything to do with Bill's death she probably is." Instinctively he decided not to wait.

When he left Winona, Detective Morrison drove directly to Bill Rhoads's offices where he spent most of the night going over papers. The one thing that struck him as being odd was the nature of the last case file Bill was working on. It was a divorce case involving a Cuban diplomat and his American wife. Then he came across something in the file that sent a cold chill down his spine.

It was a small note in Bill's handwriting that said, "Call Todd about the tail." So Bill was being followed.

And at this very moment he was reaching out to Todd from the grave. It scared the bejeezus out of him. And right now he wished he was far away from there. Far, far, away.

CHAPTER 7

Washington D.C. Nine Hours Earlier

Washington D.C. held its breath as news reports concerning the crash of the Canadian Express and the futile rescue attempts were being broadcast almost continuously over most of the TV and radio stations.

When rescuers thought they had reached someone still alive amidst what was left of the train, time and again what they found was another crushed and broken body to add to the body count. Over the past three days they had finally retrieved nearly all of the bodies from the train and had accounted for most of the names on the passenger manifest.

There were a few people still missing however so the search continued. Though without much hope of finding anyone else alive. After all, no one could have survived such an incredible disaster reporters said from the scene of the wreck.

The Perez family was more and more mentioned on the news as being among the missing and unaccounted for. And because of that, their names and faces were being broadcast around the country.

The bell rang. Adrian Perez got up from the lunch he was having and went to see who was at the door. Ever since the day after the train crashes various members of the press had constantly bothered him. As he opened the front door he saw two men standing there.

One was a young white male around thirty years or so. The other could only be described as a bull of a man. A white male about six feet two and at least two hundred and twenty pounds. It was this man who addressed Adrian. "Mr. Adrian Perez?" he asked. Adrian had the distinct feeling that these men were not from the press.

"Yes I am," he replied. "Can I help you?"

"My name is Detective Todd Morrison of the D.C. Police. May we come in?"

"Yes of course," Adrian insisted as he stepped aside to allow the men in. He led them to the living room where removing their coats the two men sat on a sofa while Adrian sat in an over large arm chair.

Adrian said to the detectives, "I guess you're here concerning my family." Both men looked at each other.

"Mr. Perez, we are sorry to hear about your wife and kids. We sincerely hope that they are found alive. But that's not why we're here today," Detective Morrison said as his partner Rick Gates took out a note pad and pencil. Adrian bolted upright in his seat and nervously looked at the two men who sat across from him. *What the hell was going on here?*

Morrison continued. "There's a chance you might be able to help us. We're doing an investigation of a hit and run and possible homicide. The victim was a private detective named Bill Rhoads who was run down in the street in front of his office."

Todd took his time. "His records show that the last person he was working for was your wife, Mr. Perez. Are you aware of that? And if so, maybe you can enlighten us."

Adrian sat very still in his chair. Well the guy following him had been a P.I. working for Beverly. He probably had taken pictures of him and Lisa together at the apartment. *Wait a minute! If this P.I. was at the apartment or in the apartment he must have found...*

So! That was how Beverly had got the information to blackmail him. The police must not have found anything yet that could incriminate him or tie him to the hit and run. He believed if they had, these gentlemen would not be sitting here asking him questions. He knew now that both Beverly and the P.I. both had documentation that would prove he was spying on the U.S. for Cuba. But they were both dead. At least he knew for sure the P.I. was.

And it was just a matter of time until they found the bodies of Beverly and the kids. But why was it taking them so long. Unless...

Adrian leaped out of his seat and yelled, "God damn it."

The two detectives looked up at him startled. "Is there something wrong Mr. Perez?" Morrison asked.

"It's just that ah... Well you see... I'm sorry gentlemen." Adrian said pulling himself together.

"It's just that I'm so distraught about my wife and children, I don't think I can continue this interview at this time. But I can tell you that I don't know anything about what Beverly may have hired this P.I. for. Now if you will excuse me..."

The two detectives got up and Morrison said, "How about if we give you a call tomorrow Mr. Perez. That'll give you some time to think about it some more and maybe you'll remember something."

Adrian walked them to the door and upon opening it smiled and said that he was sure there was nothing else to tell. Bidding them good afternoon, he shut the door quietly behind them as they left.

As the two men walked down the steps to the sidewalk and their car, detective Rick Gates said to Morrison, "What was that all about?"

Morrison replied, "That, my young fellow, was a man on the verge of panic."

"What was he so scared of?" Gates asked.

"I'm not sure, but I think it's time we gave Bill Rhoads office one more look see. And this time we take the crime lab boys along for the ride." They got in the car and drove off.

Adrian watched from the window as they pulled off and cursed under his breath. He went back into the breakfast room where his lunch had turned cold. He grabbed the plate of food and threw it against the wall and nearly yanked the wall phone out of its socket as he grabbed it, he dialed a number and then hung up.

As he went upstairs to his bedroom to change his clothes the phone rang. He picked it up and told whoever was on the line to meet him at the apartment

in one hour and hung up. He repeated this sequence
four more times before leaving the house.

Driving to the apartment, he was plagued with the
realization that the rescuers from the U.S. and Canada
would never find the bodies of his wife and children.
He was sure now that they had never been on that train
in the first place and that he had to find them before
anyone else did.

At the apartment, pest control was waiting for him.
They proceeded inside where Adrian apprised them of
the situation. After some discussion on how to proceed
they decided to first get a fax printout of Beverly's
credit card usage within the last three days, using a
special service employed by the Cuban Consul. In less
than an hour they hit the jackpot. They received a
printout on the fax machine that showed the purchase
of three Eastern Airline tickets to Orlando Florida the
same day she left the house. Now they knew where she
was. And Adrian knew that Florida was where her
brother lived.

He sent Shortwaves 1, 2, and 4 to Florida in pursuit
of Beverly and the kids. But now he had a new job for
3 and 5. He needed to keep the police off his trail for at
least 48 hours more and assigned 3 and 5 to the task.

Adrian disbursed money and travelers checks he
kept in the safe among them. It was time to leave the
apartment for good. But before they did that, Adrian
removed three containers of gasoline from the trunk of
his car and they spread two of the cans everywhere in
the apartment.

Afterwards, everyone left the apartment except Shortwave 3 who stayed behind for a few minutes to allow everyone else to get far away. He took six wooden matches and tied them around a cigarette, with the phosphor at the center of the cigarette, and tied the homemade fuse to a long rag he had previously soaked with gasoline and immersed it in the last full can of gas.

He lit the cigarette and left the apartment to get in his car which he drove about a block away and then pulled over. In about five minutes he heard the gas can explode violently and drove away.

The ensuing fire quickly spread, destroying the apartment before catching on to a number of other apartments in the same complex, trapping and killing two children and a babysitter in one apartment before firefighters could put it out.

Adrian drove back to his house and received a call from a local news reporter he had previously talked to. The reporter told him that he should know that the authorities were coming out with the story tomorrow that the Perez family had not been on the Canadian Express though a sleeping car had been reserved in their name.

No shit. He thanked the reporter for what could only be described as good news and hung up.

Shortwave 3 loved violence.

Ever since he was a kid he delighted in things violent or that were violent in nature. He had felt a certain thrill at the sound of the explosion back at the apartment that was indescribable. As he drove back to the office of the man he had run down the other day he mulled over in his mind the best way to enter the building and destroy whatever evidence he might find in the man's office.

And destroy it in such a way that would give him that special high he needed.

As he approached the building he saw, arriving at the same time, a number of police cars including a crime lab van. He drove on by them, trying to decide what to do next. He came to a decision and hurried to his own apartment. Once inside he removed a wood panel on the wall in the basement that hid a small room.

In the room were numerous weapons and explosives of all kinds. He took an empty briefcase and filled it with more of the same explosive he used on the Canadian Express, connected the timing device and set it for 45 minutes. "It will be close," he said aloud to the spiders and cobwebs as he replaced the panel and took the brief case out to the car. He got in and drove back to the office building in about thirty five minutes. By the time he got there he was shaking with excitement.

He parked about six doors from the building and from under his seat he took a berretta handgun and stuck it in his coat pocket.

Getting out of the car with the briefcase he went up the buildings steps, brazenly walking by the police sentry who only gave what he thought was a business type with a brief case a cursory glance.

Shortwave 3 stopped in the lobby checking the building index for the name Bill Rhoads. He found it listed on the second floor. Room 212. He decided to use the steps.

Detective Todd Morrison was standing just outside 212 in the hallway talking to one of the crime lab people when he noticed a man wearing an overcoat and carrying a briefcase quickly walk by and giving him a nod as he passed. His eyes followed the man as he continued on down the hallway and disappeared around the corner.

Todd turned back to the officer and continued to talk, when just as quickly the man came back down the hallway heading for the stairs. In Todd's mind, something wasn't right. Then he knew what it was. The briefcase he'd seen him carry was gone!

He yelled at the man to stop as he reached inside his jacket for his regulation 36. All the other officers inside room 212 ran out asking what had happened and Todd pointed to the man running for the stairs. Most of the officers gave chase, but Todd and the officer he had been talking to ran down the hallway in the direction the man had come from. Just around the corner lying against the wall was the briefcase.

S3 ran down the steps as fast as he could. And ran right into two astonished police officers who were on their way up to investigate all the ruckus. He pulled the berretta from his coat pocket and fired point blank in one officer's face, quickly shooting the other in the chest before he could get his weapon out.

At the sound of gunfire, the officers chasing him slowed up and cautiously proceeded down the stairs. S3 ran for the lobby where people who had heard the gunshots crouched in fear or lay down on the floor. This time the sentry outside, alerted by the gunfire, was standing just inside the front door with his weapon drawn.

As S3 came running towards him he yelled, "Stop where you are and throw down your weapon."

S3 considered all his options in a millisecond, and knew he had but one choice. Without stopping, he fired three quick shots slamming the officer in the neck and shoulder before he could return fire.

The officer fell backward down the buildings steps and on to the sidewalk before getting off his own shot just as S3 came running out the door. The bullet caught S3 in the left eye and shattered his nose before embedding itself in the wall outside.

He screamed in pain and stumbled down the steps but kept his feet under him and was able to run up the street in the direction of his car. There was no chase given because all the other officers had stopped to give aid to the wounded.

Detective Morrison who had picked up the briefcase in the hallway, made his way downstairs past everyone to the street, just as S3 drove off. He yelled for everybody to run because he was carrying a bomb. Shocked pedestrians and bystanders who had witnessed the gun battle scattered in all directions

While Morrison looked left and right not sure of what to do.

He knew there wasn't much time left because of the way S3 had hurried to get out of the building. Down the street he saw a trash truck approaching and ran for it as hard as he could waving his free arm.

He stopped the truck and told the driver he was a police officer and then ran to the back of the vehicle and threw the briefcase in the trash dump. He yelled for the driver to start the compacting mechanism and then to get out and run as fast as he could.

Waiting just long enough to see that the driver followed his instructions, he also took to his heels as fast as he could. But before he had reached a place of relative safety, the bomb exploded tearing the sides and the roof off the truck shooting trash and debris into the air and all over parked cars and pedestrians.

The shockwave from the explosion shattered cars and building windows everywhere along the street and lifted Det. Morrison off the ground before throwing him back down on the blacktop knocking him unconscious.

The entire block was in a state of bedlam. People were running and screaming. Some were in shock and a number of injured were lying on the sidewalks and street as trash filtered down from the air upon them. A few cars were involved in accidents resulting from the explosion.

But S3 had made it clear of the area before the bomb went off.

He drove along in horrible rushes of pain that threatened to sink him into unconsciousness as he held his hand over his left eye socket trying to keep the blood and gore from spilling down his face. He realized his left eye was gone and that his nose had been reduced to a mass of jelly and splintered cartilage.

He felt sure his eye was lying back there somewhere in the mayhem, but in reality it had been disintegrated by the impact of the policeman's bullet. Delirium set in as he made his way to a hospital and he began to think of the detective who had sounded the alarm.

In his state of mind he couldn't understand why the man did what he did. "The stinking bastard had no right. It certainly was his own business what he was doing there in the building." He cursed at the top of his lungs. "Why hadn't the son of a bitch minded his own? "

There he was, walking along not bothering anybody, when along comes this Sherlock Holmes, Lone Ranger lunatic with his bullshit!

Damn! His eye was really hurting now. Well... actually... not his eye. "My eye is back there on the street, probably checking out the sights and looking up dresses," he said as he began to giggle. His right eye was going to miss that sonofabitchin' left one. And just like any other right eye, it would probably start crying about it. He laughed hard and then choked on some blood in his throat.

S3 pulled into a hospital's emergency parking lot, turned the car's engine off and threw up all over himself. "Oh damn! I just had this outfit cleaned yesterday." Getting out of the car, he said to no one in particular, "Oh Mr. Detective! You and me are going to do a waltz. Yes sir, a death waltz. A good old fashion Vienna death waltz."

He laughed as he walked through the sliding double doors of the emergency waiting room where he promptly passed out onto the floor.

Detective. Morrison woke up the next morning with a terrible headache. He opened his eyes and found himself in a hospital room surrounded by flowers and potted plants. A nurse was standing by his bed checking his vital signs and his partner Rick Gates sat in a chair next to a window as the sun shone through. He was looking directly at Todd.

The nurse said, "Well I see you've finally come back to us." She reached over and pressed a silent buzzer on the wall behind him and left the room. Rick got up from the chair and walked over to the bed.

"How ya' doin' Sarge?" he whispered. "You had us worried there for a while."

Todd's mouth felt like cloth. When trying to sit up he replied, "I'm doin' about as well as can be expected, I guess. Maybe you can fill me in on what happened. How long have I been here?"

"You've been in this place since late yesterday. Do you remember anything at all?"

"Well the last thing I recall is throwing that bomb into the trash truck. I can assume it was a bomb, can't I?" Todd asked looking at Rick.

"Oh, it was a bomb all right. About 30 pounds of H 2 plastic was packed into that briefcase, or at least that's what the boys down at the lab are betting. If you hadn't disposed of it the way you did, this place could have been full of casualties and dead bodies. As it is we've got one dead cop and two lying in intensive care seriously wounded.

"And," Rick sighed, "there are about ten civilian casualties. *But* they're all minor. You know, bumps and bruises, a couple of broken bones, nothing too serious thanks to you."

"Where did all this stuff come from?" Todd asked, gesturing at all the flowers and plants.

Rick smiled and said, "Sarge you're not going to believe this, but when the news media arrived at the scene, somehow they found out that it was you who risked life and limb to save the office building and everyone in it."

"Your name and picture have been on the tube ever since. And it seems there must be a lot of people out there who want to show their gratitude because this stuff, as you like to call it, has been coming in nonstop all day. You're the biggest news since that train wreck up in Canada."

At that point a doctor entered the room followed by Todd and Rick's boss, Captain Harvey, and the head of the police department, Commissioner Whitby.

The doctor took a quick look at Todd and asked how he felt. Todd, a little abashed at the commissioner being there, said he was feeling a little better. "Good." replied the doctor, "There's a couple of people here who would like to speak to you."

"Yes. I can see," Todd said. The doctor smiled and left the room.

Captain Harvey spoke first. "Todd," he said, "you and I go way back, and I must tell you that I have never encountered a more stubborn, hardheaded, crab ass as yourself."

"Just what in the hell did you think you were doing out there. You could have gotten yourself killed. If that bomb had gone off a few seconds earlier you'd be in deep shit right now. And I'd have your ass on the carpet."

Todd wondered what the hell Bob was talking about. If that bomb had gone off a few seconds earlier he'd be dead. So out of deference to the commissioner, he was very polite when he said, "Captain Harvey sir, your holiness, what in god's name was I supposed to do?" When Bob Harvey and the commissioner started laughing, he laid back and closed his eyes, swearing softly.

The Commissioner spoke up, "Seriously Sgt. Morrison, I think I speak for a whole lot of people when I say, thank you. Just thank you." He took Todd's hand in his for a moment and then turned to Captain Harvey and said, "Make sure they take good care of this man, Captain. If he needs anything or wants anything, see that he gets it." He smiled at Todd and said, "Well I'd better go and tell that mob of reporters out there that you're going to be all right."

He straightened his tie, and looking at Todd, he asked, "How do I look, Sergeant?"

Todd replied, "Duke you're ready for the Mayor's office, sir."

The Commissioner howled with laughter, "You bet Sarge, You bet." And left the room still laughing.

Rick Gates joined Captain Harvey by Todd's bedside. Todd sat all the way up in bed and looked at the Captain. "Bob, what's the line on our shooter?"

"Terrorist is more like it." Bob replied. "A real professional. He was definitely sent there to put your lights out for good! And unfortunately he got away.

But one of the officers he shot got a good look at him."
That same officer was able to return fire and is 100
percent certain that Mr. Dynamite is suffering pretty
bad right now around the head area. So we're running a
check of all the hospitals in town to see if they received
any head wound emergencies in the past 24 hours."

"It's about the best we can do right now, Todd. Too
bad the son of a bitch got away."

Todd thought for a moment. In the back of his
mind, he had a pretty good idea who was behind it all.
"Captain, how soon can I get out of here?" he asked.

"Well, the doc said, barring any complications, that
tomorrow morning will be soon enough. They just
want to keep you under observation a little while
longer since you were out cold for more than 18
hours."

Todd looked at his friend sheepishly. "You know, I
got a good look at him, too," Todd insisted. "So if I
have to be stuck in here, it wouldn't do any harm if I
looked at some mug shots. After all, the Commissioner
did say..."

"Yea, yea, I know what the Commissioner said."

Captain Harvey threw his hands up in the air, "I
give up. Detectives." he said, "Try to talk some sense
into him." He shook Todd's hand and left the room.

Rick stood over his partner and said, "You know
he's right. You should try and get some rest..."

Todd breathed out slowly and yawned. "Maybe
you're right, ole buddy," he said, "maybe you're right."
He closed his eyes. Before long he was sleeping
peacefully, and Rick Gates smiled down at him before
turning off the light as he left the room.

CHAPTER 8

Philadelphia PA, Sunday 10 p.m.

Ray Williams was tired. He had been trying most of the evening to raise station WCZX, his old friend Charlie Wells, in Ohio, but without any luck. His ham radio seemed to be working just fine and interference with reception was not a factor on this particular night.

Charlie and Marlon must be out living it up, Ray thought with a chuckle. After all, tomorrow was their tenth wedding anniversary. After some thought, he decided to listen in on an open frequency for a while before turning in for the night.

After a few minutes of fiddling with the beat frequency oscillator (BFO) and squelch knobs and not recognizing any call signature known to him, he was just about to shut down when over the speaker came a faint and garbled voice. Ray adjusted the radio until he could make out what was being said. Then he heard it.

He listened a couple minutes to make sure of what he was hearing and softly called to his wife Debora who was just in the other room making the bed.

"Hey Deb, you better come here. I'm gonna' need your help."

Deborah Williams immediately stopped what she was doing. She had learned, after eight years of marriage, to respond immediately when her husband, who was blind from birth, needed her. She quickly walked into the pigpen. That's what they called the extra bedroom where Ray kept his ham radio and other assorted things he collected.

Hearing her come in, Ray said, "Listen to this, hon." As he turned up the speaker she could hear the voice of a little girl who could not have been more than ten.

"Can somebody hear me?"

"Somebody please talk to me. My mommy's been shot and so is my brother. The boat's on a rock in the ocean and it's... it's... dark outside. Somebody talk to me please. Please help me."

Ray and Deborah could hear the girl start to cry. "Oh my God." said Deborah as she squeezed Ray's shoulder, "Oh my God."

The Caribbean

Sunday 10:20 p.m.

Jennifer Perez wiped the tears from her eyes and wondered if anyone could really hear her. She had seen the captain turn on the radio and speak into the microphone numerous times during the trip, but she wasn't really sure if she was doing it right. She wanted to go up on deck to see if she could see anything, but not only was she scared of the dark, her mother and brother were up there and that was more frightening than anything. Suddenly she heard a voice on the radio. "Hello. Hello there, we can hear you. This is station WEAX in Philadelphia. What is your name and the name of your boat! Over."

Jennifer was shaking all over and had a difficult time replying, but soon said. "My name is Jennifer, and I'm on a fishing boat. I think it's called the Angel." Then she said, "Over." Just like she had seen the captain do and released the mike switch.

"Jennifer, my name is Ray Williams. My wife Deborah and I are going to try and help you. Can you tell us approximately where you are? Over."

"I don't know," answered Jennifer. "We were fishing, and we found another boat, and... we thought it was broke... but then these men and..." Jennifer started to cry again and dropped the radio mike.

"This is going to be more difficult than it seems." Ray said to Deborah. "You'd better get on the phone and see if you can't reach the Coast Guard facility down at Penn's Landing. There must be someone there. Even if it is Sunday night."

Jennifer realized that she had dropped the mike and picked it up because Ray was talking to her again. Speaking as soothingly as possible he continued. "Listen Jennifer there are a few things I need for you to do. Okay? Over."

He heard a soft "Yes, over," from Jennifer.

"First of all, I want you to stay on this frequency as long as you can. Do you understand that? Over."

He was rewarded with another soft, "Yes."

"Good. Now secondly, can you think of anything that might tell me where you are? Anything at all. Over"·

Ray asked Deborah if they were shooting in the dark at this point. "The child has already said she didn't know where she was, and after all she said she'd been through, it is a wonder she isn't in shock by now." Ray said.

Deborah replied, "She was able to make a distress call, and that means that this little girl is not ready to throw it all in."

After a few seconds Jennifer replied. "We're on vacation. I. I. mean we were on vacation, over."

"Where, Jennifer? Where are you on vacation? Over."

"The Bahamas. We're... in ... the Bahamas..." she replied weakly.

"Good, Jennifer, Very good," Ray said, smiles crossed his and Deborah's faces.

"Now can you tell me where in the Bahamas, Jennifer?

"Nassau? Maybe Paradise Island?" He suggested trying to help her remember. But this time there was no reply.

"Jennifer can you hear me? Over." Jennifer would not hear him again.

She had calmly put the mike down, slowly curled up on one of the bunks in the cabin and closed her eyes.

The deadly events of the day had finally taken hold of her, and she had retreated to a place far away. A place where the men could not bring their guns and cause so much pain and death; a place where she might find peace. But terribly a place where Ray and Deborah Williams could no longer reach her.

And the Angel, a charter fishing boat registered out of Palm Bay Florida, to a Captain Paul Stokes, had come to rest on a desolate coral reef about 30 nautical miles southwest of the Grand Bahamas after drifting for more than six hours.

She stood stranded and alone. Of her four passengers, two were dead and two more soon could be. For in the eastern night sky, dark and ominous storm clouds rumbled a warning of things to come, as a strong breeze began to blow watery whitecaps; seen only by one or two gulls quickly seeking refuge in some distant haven.

CHAPTER 9

U.S. Coast Guard Cutter:

The Harpoon, Somewhere in the Caribbean. 11:30 p.m.

The U.S. Coast Guard is an often maligned branch of the military service, thought F.B.I. agent Jim Green, as he flipped through the Department of Defense brochure he'd received prior to his assignment aboard the Harpoon. Not only did they enforce maritime law and assist vessels wrecked, or in distress, on or near the coasts, but they could also be responsible for the maintenance of lighthouses, buoys, and other navigational aids; and for administering emergency aid to merchant seamen and to victims of natural disasters, such as floods and hurricanes as they did in New Orleans when Katrina hit.

The Coast Guard's collection and dissemination of meteorological data pertaining to floods and storms alone made it the most active branch of the military service. Not to mention, the support it afforded all the law enforcement agencies including, but not withstanding the C.I.A., The E.P.A, Bureau of Tobacco and Firearms, Customs, and his employer the F.B.I.

Jim put the brochure down and looked around his cramped quarters. There was an upper and lower bunk, in which he had chosen the latter. Two small lockers barely large enough to hold one person's gear, let alone two, were fastened against the forward bulkhead. To complete the picture, a small desk with a little chair underneath stood next to a tight hatchway that led the passageway outside. A light switch next to the hatchway provided the finishing touch. *This was not the presidential suite at the Watergate in Washington D.C., but it will have to do.*

During the next forty-eight hours, this ship would be his home. He had come aboard the Harpoon at 6 p.m. and was immediately briefed about the combined air and sea drug bust that was to take place somewhere in Bahamian waters around 6 p.m. tomorrow. After being shown his quarters, the ship had left dock for the open sea.

Since this was a joint military venture between the U.S. and the Bahamas, his status on board was as an observer. But if all their information attained after months of back breaking investigation proved to be solid, his quarry, Ruiz Alvarez, would be somewhere out there waiting for a drop. And as pre-arranged, once caught he was to be arrested by the U.S. Coast Guard. Until such time as they re-entered American waters. At which time he would be able to take Alvarez into custody. "Well I've waited this long to meet the man, I guess I can wait a few more hours," he said aloud.

Jim noticed his stomach was growling and realized he had not eaten since the flight from Washington to

Miami earlier that afternoon. All they had at the Miami bureau, which he briefly visited, was coffee and donuts.

Stretching his six foot 170 pound frame, he yawned and got up from his bunk making his way to the passageway and after a few wrong turns found the galley.

He was surprised to see a number of sailors sitting around talking and having what could only be a late dinner. He took a tray from a rack and walked up to the counter where a Mess Chief was supervising the dishing out of hot food. "Hey, Cookie," he said, "What's on the menu?"

In reply he got, "Who the hell you calling Cookie, ya creep." Some of the men seated at the tables broke out in laughter.

"Whoa! Hold on now," Jim said, "I didn't mean to ruffle your feathers."

The cook said, "If anyone's got feathers, it's you, bird brain!" Everybody laughed then. Jim held his hands up in surrender. And the cook, with a scowl on his face, served him. On his tray he placed a huge cut of prime rib, a baked potato with a dollop of butter, a ladle of mixed vegetables, and two hot buttered rolls.

"Boy, this really looks delicious." Jim tried to humor the cook.

The cook said, "How would you know?"

"What do you mean?" Jim said, knowing he wasn't going to like the answer.

"Well, what I mean is, just how can anybody see anything with their head stuck up their ass." Everybody howled at that, and Jim hurriedly found a corner in which he could hide. He sat down at an empty table and was almost finished eating when an ensign he met earlier at the briefing, walked into the galley and over to his table.

"May I join you?" he questioned.

"Sure. Why not?" said Jim. "There doesn't seem to be a line forming up for seats at this table."

The ensign laughed, taking a seat. "I heard what happened. Look," he said, "don't take the Mess Chief too seriously. It's just his way of making all new personnel feel at home."

I'm glad to hear that," said Jim feeling a little relieved but not much.

"Listen as soon as you're ready Captain Dunn would like to see you up on the bridge. I'll be seeing you soon." And with that he was up and gone. Jim quickly finished what was left of dinner and got up to leave. The galley was almost empty now except for one man having coffee. Jim got out of there as quick as he could and soon found himself outside on deck. It was a warm night, and Jim breathed in the tropical air. *We must be well out of the Florida Keys by now.*

It was really quite nice. He always loved boats, and as a child had often gone sailing with his father on the Potomac. He climbed up the ladder to the bridge and was greeted by Captain Dunn. "Well, there you are, Mister Green," he said as Jim entered the bridge. "Nice to have you aboard."

Jim smiled as he shook his hand and took a moment to view his surroundings. The bridge was bathed in soft multi-colored light emanating from a vast array of state of the art and highly technical communication and navigational equipment. "This is some ship, Captain."

"Yes, we have all the latest gadgets the tax payers' money can buy," Dunn said with a chuckle. Jim pointed to what looked like a large picture frame without the picture mounted on a computer.

"What is that if I might ask?" said Jim quizzically.

"Why, that's our pride and joy, Mister Green. That is our new land sat. It operates under the same principle as most land to satellite navigational devices but with a couple new twists."

"What are they?" Jim asked.

"Well first of all, not only do we use it to tell exactly where we are at all times, but this screen you see here is what's called a holo-signal modulator. Say you have a ship lost at sea. What this unit does is causes a signal to bounce off the appropriate satellite at a thousand times a second, creating a blanket hologram that can show any inanimate object on the water, larger than a nickel, mind you, within a fifteen hundred mile radius."

"Whew, that's pretty impressive," Jim said. "But let me ask you this..."

"Go ahead," the captain said with a smile.

"Suppose you find you have a hundred boats on your screen, how can you tell which one is the one you're looking for?"

"Well the satellite takes a close up picture of each ship along with the land sat co-ordinates and instantaneously sends them back to the modulator which then digitally reproduces each ship in 3-D until it can read the name of each one. The computer makes a list of all the names, we key in the name of the ship we're looking for and get a picture and the location. The whole process takes a little less than thirty minutes."

Jim whistled softly. "That's incredible," he said.

"Now I have something to tell you, Jim, if you don't mind me calling you Jim." Jim insisted that he didn't.

"About an hour ago we got a message from southern command to do a holo-scan, I like to call it. They got a relay from Coast Guard station N 12 up north concerning the likelihood of a distress call, coming from a boat called the Angel in the area of the Bahamas."

"Seems some ham operator picked it up and reported it. Strange though how no one else did. Since we were headed that way they called us.

"And as instructed we did a scan of each of the major Bahaman Islands outside five miles of landfall so we wouldn't pick up boats in harbors or natural anchorages." Captain Dunn turned to the sailor at the console. "Put it up on the screen, seaman."

As if by magic a gray-blue picture of a boat materialized in the air inside the frame.

As it rotated on its axis, Jim could see the name, Angel, plainly written at the bow. Under the picture floated the co-ordinates 24-77-5. "We now know that a boat with this name and fitting this description radioed its departure from the Bahamas this morning and hasn't been seen or heard from since. Therefore, I have been ordered to reconnoiter and assist in this matter, but don't worry because we won't miss tomorrow's party. I just felt you should be made aware of the situation, so just sit back and enjoy the ride."

Jim left the bridge after thanking the captain and climbed down to the deck. He stood at the railing and watched the dark water go by below. The wind had picked up, and he wondered if there wasn't a storm brewing somewhere in the night sky.

He thought momentarily about Ruiz Alvarez and the drug ring he operated. But his real concern was about the strange rescue mission they were about to embark upon. His instincts told him that it would be much more than just a rescue. And that somehow the Angel would play a greater role in the scheme of things.

Jim had a strange dream that night. Reminiscent of a conversation heard during dinner. He dreamed he was a seaman aboard an ice breaker in the arctic where the Coast Guard's International Ice Patrol kept the fishing lanes free from icebergs and floes. In his dream, a little girl was drowning beneath the ice and somehow he could hear her chilling cry, "The Angel is dead. The Angel is dead."

He could see her face as she struggled to reach out for him. But the ship was being heaved away by huge mountains of ice. He watched as the little girl sank down into the depths. In his dream he found himself diving through ice covered seas and swimming down into the darkness where he felt the little girl grasp his hand. A sense of peace washed over him as he began to swim for the surface in his dream. Suddenly, he was awakened by the repeated blast of the Harpoon's morning call to reveille.

Jim sat up in his bunk and immediately felt the ship pitch and roll and knew the weather had changed. After getting his sea legs, he showered and dressed before reporting to the stateroom for the 0715 briefing. Finding a seat, he noticed that all officers and crewmen seemed to be there and wondered who was running the ship. Captain Dunn entered the room, and everyone came to attention.

During the first order of business his earlier concern about the weather was confirmed. It had changed dramatically overnight, and they were feeling the first effects of a tropical storm called Sarah.

For the next twenty minutes or so the talk turned to tactics, and Jim had some time to think about what had led him to be here. His career with the F.B.I. started six years ago, and he had joined the bureau after first being a correctional officer for three years in the Maryland state prison system and then doing a stint as a U.S. Marshal for five years.

Earlier on, coming out of high school, he had acquired a 2nd degree black belt in Tang Soo Do and had actively sought admittance to the Air Force Academy.

But being from a working class family, he didn't have the resources, or the congressional sponsorship, necessary for acceptance. He never blamed anyone and considered it a matter for fate to decide. As far as he was concerned he had come a long way. The F.B.I. considered him one of their brightest and best special agents. He was proud of that fact.

Whatever he lacked in knowledge he could have gotten at the college level, he more than made up in hard work and long hours. He often accepted assignments that other agents may have balked at because of family considerations, age, or what have you. Though lately, he had been thinking that maybe it was time he found someone to settle down with.

But it wasn't easy at the age of thirty-five. Especially when most women wanted someone they could change. He had been a challenge for more than one. Inevitably though, it always wound up the same way, both parties trying to find a way to call it off without hurting one another's feelings. Here there was regret, and his mind turned to Ruiz Alvarez.

Jim had been at the F.B.I. a little more than four years when he first came across the Alvarez file. There was nothing initially to set it apart from the usual type of kingpin cases. So it had been assigned to him on a non-priority basis.

Ruiz Alvarez seemed to be a small time trafficker of cocaine and marijuana with mob connections. Intelligence sources said he ran his operation out of an apartment in Washington D.C., but surveillance teams couldn't catch him at it.

For more than a year they kept coming up dry. Until one day Jim decided to try cross referencing pictures and finger prints taken after all drug busts in the continental U.S. over a twelve month period, with known associates of Alvarez. And bingo! He made a connection.

Hector Ramus, a man who matched the description of a known visitor to the D.C. apartment, had been arrested by customs agents in Miami while trying to smuggle a small amount of heroin into the U.S. via the Bahamas. He had been arraigned and released after a few hours, on a five thousand dollar bond, and promptly disappeared.

Usually this would have merited only a warrant of arrest in Miami. But Jim felt that it was extremely unusual that heroin would be the substance found on him at the time. He shelved the warrant and got a sample of the heroin from customs.

Chemical analysis proved it to be more than 90 percent pure, and it didn't end there. First, after backtracking Hectors' whereabouts in the Bahamas, it was discovered that he had flown into Nassau on a private plane from Cuba. Alarm bells went off everywhere in the bureau, even at the front office.

But when the fingerprints taken at the arrest in Miami confirmed that Hector Ramus was an alias and cover for one Ruiz Alvarez, all hell broke loose. Jim was given top priority and had access to anyone and anything he needed. He proved more than up to the task.

Two months later his investigation finally revealed the long pipeline that Alvarez had created. He was buying large quantities of raw opium in Pakistan, which was being transported overland by pack mules and then by boat to Cuba. It was being flown over the Bahamas and dropped to him and his small fleet of fishing boats waiting in international waters at prearranged locations. It had taken a few more months to pinpoint exactly where the drops were being made and to set up Alvarez.

Jim knew that Alvarez's people in the U.S. were being arrested at that very moment and that it was imperative that he be stopped before he could get away. It was now believed that the heroin confiscated in Miami had only been a sample for prospective buyers in the U.S. and that his real supply was somewhere in the Bahamas.

Jim heard his name being called.

"And this is special agent, Jim Green, of the F.B.I.," Jim heard the captain say, pointing in his direction. "So feel free to extend him a helping hand if he needs it." Jim casually waved to the men around him. "Now, unless there's some other business, this meetings at an end. Don't forget, we will reach the area of the Angel at around 1000 hours, so I want all divers in wet gear ready to move out by that time."

Someone called "Attention," and everyone stood up as Captain Dunn left the state room. Feeling famished, Jim went down to the galley and had breakfast to order. It consisted of a huge stack of flapjacks with syrup and butter, which he used freely, three eggs over easy, and six strips of bacon washed down with cups of steaming coffee and some orange juice.

The Mess Chief who had tongue lashed him the night before wasn't on duty and was glad of it. As he finished breakfast, he wondered what they would find when they reached the Angel and the Alvarez drop as it was being called. *Would the weather be a factor? Would they find anything at all?* He just didn't know. And wondered if anyone really did.

CHAPTER 10

The Caribbean:

Aboard the Harpoon, 1000 Hours

Jim Green was in his cabin when the all-hands-on-deck call was given. He donned the wet gear he had received upon boarding and joined the rest of the crew. The Harpoon reeled under the full force of Tropical Storm Sarah when Jim reached the deck. A few crewmembers were handing out life preservers, and Jim took one and put it on. The rain was coming down in sheets and the deck was slippery. The wind was blowing so hard it was difficult to keep a steady balance.

Jim literally had to fight his way through the maelstrom to reach the bridge. Upon entering, he removed his rain parka and noted the bridge was busy with activity. Captain Dunn said, "Nice weather we're having, isn't it?" He smiled.

A sailor looked up from the radar and said, "Captain, the target is now approximately five hundred yards off the port bow."

The Captain said, "Helmsman 30 decrees to port side."

"Aye aye, Captain, 30 degrees to port side," he replied.

"Come on Angel, where are you?" Captain Dunn said to no one in particular as he viewed the horizon through field glasses. After a few minutes the Angel came into view through the pouring rain. She was about fifty yards dead ahead and on her starboard side as storm swells picked her up and dropped her down onto the reef.

"Helmsman, point her into the wind. All engines neutral," the Captain said. A seaman echoed his command.

"First mate, deploy the sea anchor."

The first mate said, "Aye aye Captain, deploying the sea anchor," and left the bridge.

The Captain spoke into the ship's loud speaker. "Rescue crew and divers deploy lifeboats 1 and 2."

Jim watched as the men on deck released the lifeboats into the water. One of the boats was washed back on deck by a huge wave that broke over the side of the ship. The men struggled to get the boat back in the water and under control. The rescue crew and the divers finally got under way.

As they made their way across the distance between the two vessels, the divers could see the dark reef in the water below. About thirty feet from the Angel, the reef came dangerously close to the surface and they could go no further.

The three divers exited the boat they were in and made their way to the Angel, half swimming and half walking over the reef. They had to be extremely careful because the sea swells were also lifting them up and dropping them back down onto the reef. A loss of balance could mean severe injury or death. When they reached the Angel, one of the divers called out for anyone who would hear.

Getting no response, each diver carefully timed their approach to the ladder at the bow of the boat with the sea swells and in a few minutes, all three divers were aboard the Angel. The first thing they saw were three bodies lying on the deck of the boat. Each one had multiple bullet wounds.

One was an older male, one a boy about thirteen or fourteen, and a woman thirty-five to forty years old. Checking for signs of life, they found the two males to be dead. But the woman was still alive. Barely.

She had a very low pulse and her heartbeat was little more than a flutter. One of the divers got back in the water as the other two lifted the woman and passed her down to him. Then another diver also got back into the water, and they both began to work their way back to the lifeboats with the woman in tow between them.

The third diver remained at the bow of the Angel until his companions had reached the boats. He could see them get the woman aboard one while a crew member began to administer oxygen to her. Seeing the boat head back towards Harpoon, he began to explore the rest of the Angel. There were no more bodies to be seen anywhere on the outside decks, and he checked the cabin. As he entered through the small teak door, he could hear talking coming from the shortwave radio inside, but more importantly was the little girl he found curled up on one of the forward bunks.

Hurrying to her side, he checked for a pulse then breathed a sigh of relief. The little girl was alive but unconscious. He went to the radio, picked up the hand mike and said, "This is the U.S. Coast Guard aboard the Angel. Is there someone on this frequency? Over."

From the speaker came the reply, "Yes! Yes! We've been here all night. Thank God you're there. Over."

"Who are you?" the diver asked.

"This is station WEAX in Philadelphia. Last night we were talking to a little girl at that end named Jennifer, but she disappeared off the air. Is she okay? Over."

The diver reacted. "Are you the people who called one of our stations up north? Over."

"Yes we are," replied Ray Williams.

"Then you'll be glad to know the little girl is still alive," answered the diver."

"Thank God," said Ray. "Thank God." Just then the other two divers who had returned to the boat entered the cabin. The diver said, "We must clear this frequency now, sir. This is a code red emergency. Someone will be contacting you. Over and out."

He turned to a frequency the Harpoon was monitoring and made a status report before they picked up the girl and left the cabin.

Two of the divers ferried the girl out to the lifeboats as before, and one remained behind to await the removal of the two bodies.

Jim Green stood on the deck of the Harpoon when the lifeboat carrying the little girl approached the ship.

As the diver holding the little girl was reaching out for a handhold, another huge wave broke over the ship and slammed him into the hull knocking him unconscious. Both he and the girl fell into the water.

Jim was one of a number of men who immediately jumped into the water. He swam down to where they had gone under and grabbed the unconscious diver by the back of his wet suit. The little girl reach out for his hand. He grabbed it and swam to the surface pulling up both of them in the process.

Jennifer held on to him for dear life.

When she had fallen into the sea she regained consciousness and started swallowing water. When she saw Jim she reached for him just like in her dream.

Many hands were lifting them out of the water and aboard the Harpoon, and presently they were taken to the ship's sickbay.

Once there Jim was checked over and released though the diver had suffered a mild concussion and would be there sometime before he was back on duty.

Jennifer vomited up a little seawater, but otherwise was all right. She became hysterical when Jim tried to leave the sickbay. He had saved her and she did not want to have him leave her side. He had to stay with her until the sedative they gave her took effect and she went to sleep. He went to his cabin and took a shower before he also fell asleep in his bunk.

In Philadelphia, Deborah Williams helped her husband Ray get into bed. He had stayed by his ham radio all night long in hopes that somehow he could still help that little girl all alone out there.

He said to Deborah as he closed his eyes, "She's okay, Deb. Did you hear what they said? They said she was okay."

Deborah lay down beside him and said, "Yes. I know, honey. I know." And quietly began to cry.

Jim was awakened at 3 p.m. He put on some clothes and went to the galley for a late lunch. Behind the counter again was the grizzled old chief cook's mate who served him the previous night.

Oh Shit! he thought. But this time the chief was extremely cordial.

"And how are we today, sir?" he said to Jim with a huge smile on his face.

"Fine chief," Jim replied.

"What'll it be?" the chief asked. Jim looked at the food and decided upon meatloaf with mashed potatoes and gravy and sweet peas.

As the chief dished the food onto his tray, he said, "I want to thank you for what you did out there today. That young fella's life you saved is my sister's son. And well, I just can't tell you what it means to me. Not to mention what you did for that little girl, too." He pointed behind Jim and said, "Here she is now."

When Jennifer had awoken earlier in the sickbay, the ship's corpsman had examined her and finding her fit as a fiddle, thought it best that she not remain there in the sickbay while her mother was fighting to stay alive. She would be staying in a cabin next to Jim's for the duration of the trip and a corpsman, after having scavenged some dry clothes for her to wear, brought her into the galley for some lunch.

When Jennifer saw Jim she ran to him and hugged him at the waist, crying. Through the tears she said. "I knew you would come. I waited for you until you came." She looked up at him.

Jim didn't know what to do. He held his tray of food in one arm and the other he put attentively around her shoulder. He led her to a table where they sat down while the corpsman got her something to eat. After she was able to compose herself, Jennifer said to Jim, "I had a dream about you. I was drowning in the darkness and you came to save me. I could have died," she said, biting her lower lip. "But I refused to because I knew you would come."

Jim said, "They say your name is Jennifer? Is that correct?" Jennifer nodded. He continued, "Well Jennifer, this may sound a little crazy, but I also had a dream and it seems to have been a lot like yours."

They continued to converse while they ate. Jim asked her if she wanted to talk about what happened aboard the Angel, and Jennifer said that if he wanted her to she would. Jim told the corpsman to get Captain Dunn. While they waited, he told Jennifer about his dream. She smiled after he finished. When Captain Dunn arrived he sat down at the table, and Jennifer began to recount the events of the past two weeks.

Jennifer sat thoughtfully for a few moments, trying not to be afraid, so she could remember as much as she could. Finally after a few minutes, she took a deep breath and began to speak "Well… when the plane landed in Orlando, we got off and went to get our stuff from baggage claim. When we got outside that's when

I saw a man sitting in a truck who looked just like our mother.

"He was her brother, Paul Stokes." Jennifer vaguely remembered Uncle Paul. He had moved to Florida, when she was still very young, to pursue his dream of owning a fishing boat business. "As soon as he got out the truck he gave Mom and me big hugs. But John just stood by with a dumb look on his face. It was like he was angry or something. We put all the stuff in the truck and got in. He told us we were headed for his home in Palm Bay. He said it was fifty miles away.

"On the way, mother told him all the stuff that happened since he left. He said that he understood about Dad and since Paul was single, his home would be their home from now on. He also told us how nice it would be to have a couple of beautiful ladies around the house, and since there was a school just down the road, we could start attending as soon as we were ready.

"John got mad and said that he wasn't ready to go to school, but mom said that it was all right. They would make a holiday of it for a couple of weeks then see what happened after that.

Jennifer asked if she could stop for a while. Everyone agreed and after a few minutes she recounted the rest of her story.

She said that after arriving in Palm Bay, they found Uncle Paul's house to be very nice. It was a stone and oak split level with four bedrooms and three baths overlooking the Indian River Lagoon. "He kept the fishing boat, he called it the Angel, out back at his private dock about twenty yards from the house. Every morning at about 7 am, he went across the river to Pirates Cove Marina where he worked.

"They said Uncle Paul was one of the most popular Captains in the area and was booked weeks in advance because people kept coming back to go fishing with him. He smiled at us and said, 'If Captain Stokes couldn't find where the fish were, nobody could,'" she said.

"After a day of getting our stuff put away, Mom asked us what we wanted to do. John said he didn't care, but I always wanted to go to Walt Disney World, so off we went." For the next couple of days they stayed at a Walt Disney hotel where a monorail picked them up in the lobby and took them to the various locations within the Disney theme park. They returned to Palm Bay afterwards and decided to visit Sea World and Cape Canaveral.

"John didn't want to go to Sea World and Cape Canaveral with us and Mom got mad. So we let him stay home the days we went.

"After about a week Uncle Paul told us a deep sea fishing charter had been canceled. He looked at the three of us with a big smile and said he had been wanting to take his boat on a trip to the Bahamas and now was as good a time as any to take it. John didn't want to go, but at the last minute changed his mind. So we filled the boat with food and bottles of water and sodas. Mom packed cloths and swim suits for us, and we left early the next morning for what Uncle Paul said would be Nassau and Paradise Island.

"It took us all day to reach Nassau where we stayed for the night.

"Uncle Paul took us to a place to eat he knew about and had been to before. We had Snapper fish, hop and johns and conch salad and papaya ice cream for dessert. The next morning we left for an island called Abaco where we spent the next three days in a beautiful lagoon.

"We spent the days laying in the sun or swimming and snorkeling in the pretty blue waters around the boat. Every night we paddled to the village for dinner at one of the restaurants. Did you know the places to eat had no walls?" Later at night back on the Angel they would listen to Bahamian music on the shortwave radio that Uncle Paul often used.

"By now even John was more fun to be with. The island people were kind to us so we hated to leave, but on the fourth day we left for the Grand Bahamas.

"That night we talked about what happened back home. John started to talk and cry then. He told us that he realized that our father was a bad man. He finally broke down in tears, and he sat out on the deck watching the stars.

"That night, as we went to bed, I thought this week on the boat so far had been the best time I had ever had and went to sleep listening to Uncle Paul and Mom talk late into the night.

"The next day we decided to go deep sea fishing and headed out to sea. After a few hours we came across a boat. It seemed to be stranded out on the ocean. When we pulled up we could see a man on board waving his arms as if signaling for help. Uncle Paul told me to go down into the cabin and stay there until he called me.

"I thought I would play a trick while I was down there and hide in the life preserver compartment I had discovered the day before. I was just small enough to fit inside and giggled at what they would think when they couldn't find me."

From there the Captain and Todd pieced together the a scenario based on what Jennifer could hear from her hiding place.

With Beverly and John on deck, Paul sided the Angel up next to the stranded boat, and the man said aloud, "Boy' Thanks a lot our gas gauge must be broke because we ran out of gas early this morning."

Paul took one of the two spare gas containers he kept strapped down at the rear of the Angel and with the help of John, handed it over to the man who said thanks and offered them some money in return.

But Paul refused it. Then the other man said, "Well at least tell me your names so I can thank you properly."

"Paul said, "I'm Captain Paul Stokes. This is my sister Beverly and my nephew, John."

The man said, "Well now, if that don't beat all. I've been looking for you people all day." And with that he whistled sharply and two other men with automatic rifles in their hands, jumped out of their hiding places on the deck of their boat and opened fired at the Angel.

The automatic fire caught Paul in the upper chest and head killing him instantly. John was pierced by bullets in the chest and neck severing his spine before falling to the deck where he died a few minutes later. Beverly was shot in the head, the right .arm, and right side and fell to the deck unconscious. The three men quickly boarded the Angel while one man opened up the other container of gas and spread it over the Angels deck and the fallen bodies, another checked the boats cabin. Jennifer was in a state of confusion. She could not see what was going on, but the sound of gunfire and thumps on the deck made the hair on her neck stand up.

She didn't know if she should come out of her hiding place or if there was anything she could do to help. But then her instincts told her to stay very quiet where she was. She heard someone enter the cabin, and she closed her eyes real tight and covered her mouth. She could tell that the person had started to look through things.

For what seemed an eternity, there was an eerie silence. She didn't think she would be able to stand it any longer when someone yelled something from outside and the person who was inside thumped out of the cabin.

In less than a minute she could hear the other boat take off at a fast rate of speed, but she still remained in her hiding place until she felt it was really safe to come out. A long time passed when she finally ventured outside the tiny compartment.

She called, "Mom? Uncle Paul? John?"

When she didn't hear anyone answer she went up on deck only to find her family lying in pools of blood. The entire deck reeked of gasoline and the sun had set.

She yelled and screamed for help, but for miles around there was nothing but water. Afraid to touch her mother, brother and uncle, sure that they were dead, she went back to the cabin and sat down on the sofa not quite sure what to do. Finally realizing the engines were still running, she went pass the bodies on deck up to the Captain's chair and turned the engine key off. She went back down to the cabin and lay down on the sofa and waited.

After a while she found she had drifted off to sleep and dreamed of a man who would come to save her.

Yet when she woke up it was around nine in the evening and no one had come and it was dark outside. Too dark and scary. So she got up and turned on the shortwave radio and began to turn the dials like she had seen her uncle do.

She called for help, finally reaching Ray Williams. Here she ended her story.

Captain Dunn and Jim Green looked at each other. Captain Dunn said to Jennifer; "Jennifer, your mother is still alive but, injured badly. But I'm afraid that I have bad news about your uncle and brother. They were dead long before we could do anything to help them."

"Is my mother in the hospital?"

"Yes, she is."

"Where is she? Can I see her?"

"I'm afraid you can't see her right now," the Captain said. "You see, she's very sick, and she needs all the rest she can if she's to get better.

"But don't worry. Because of all the many different things we are called upon to do, the Harpoon is literally a self-contained floating town. We have a very good ship's corpsman not to mention medics who are on duty twenty-four hours a day if need be. And the sickbay is state of the art. We are set up here to treat everything from a mosquito bite to shock trauma. Do you understand?"

"Yes, I think so." Jennifer gulped.

She started to cry again. "Where are my brother and uncle? Are they in the hospital with my mom?"

"No Jennifer, we have them in a special room where they are safe until we arrive back at our base," the corpsman explained. The corpsman rose from the table to take her to her room, but she wailed that she wanted to stay with Jim.

Jim spoke to the corpsman, "Where's she staying?"

"Right next to your room, sir."

"Good. I'll take her down, if it's okay with you."

The corpsman nodded okay.

Captain Dunn patted Jim on the shoulder and smiled, "Looks like you've got a big fan there, Jim."

"By the way you did quite a job out there saving this girl and Ensign Peters."

So that was his name.

"If you were in the Coast Guard, I would have to put you in for a commendation."

Jim laughed. Thinking for a moment, he became serious. "Listen," he said to Dunn; "How is this going to affect our rendezvous with Alvarez?"

"Not in the least Jim. We still expect to reach the drop off vicinity say approximately 1700 hours."

Jim looked at his watch and said, "That's about an hour from now."

"Correct. So I'd better be going now."

Dunn stood and looked at Jennifer. "You're quite a young lady," he said and turned and walked out of the galley.

Jim asked her if she was finished eating and saying she was, he took her down to the level where they were staying. Once he got her situated in her cabin and assured her he would be right next door, he left her to her own devices and went into his own cabin.

From his storage locker he pulled out one of his bags, unlocked it and removed a Sig Sauer P 220 combat pistol, which he field stripped and lightly wiped off before reassembling it, strapping it to his hip. Putting on his wet gear, he stopped at Jennifer's cabin to tell her he had to go to see the Captain and would send somebody down to look after her.

He went on deck and found the weather had changed for the better. Again he ascended to the bridge and found Captain Dunn waiting for him. "Well," said Dunn, "here we go with round two."

"Captain, could you send someone down to keep an eye on Jennifer?"

"Gladly, Mr. Green."

Dunn picked up a phone and spoke for a minute before hanging up. He turned to Jim and said, "We've picked up some activity in the approximate area of the Alvarez drop. I've already had the Formula 1 put in the water and the Bahamian Navy should arrive on schedule at 1630 hours. With them are two more fast boats and a helicopter just in case. Now I know that your status here up to this point has been as an observer," Dunn said with a gleam in his eye that made Jim wonder just what he was up to, "but you seem to be able to think pretty quick on your feet and could be of great benefit to this mission in an operational capacity. So I've taken the liberty of talking to Washington and having you temporarily appointed to my command for the duration of the mission." He took two telexes from his shirt pocket and handed them over to Jim.

One was from the Department of Defense, and it confirmed his appointment to the U.S. Coast Guard with the temporary rank of Chief Warrant Officer 2nd class until such time as the present mission was completed. At that time his commission would be deactivated to inactive status for six years.

Damn! He wasn't positive, but it certainly looked like he had somehow been shanghaied into the Coast Guard.

Captain Dunn must have pulled some big time strings at the Pentagon! He eyed the Captain quizzically who responded by roaring with laughter.

The second telex was from F.B.I. headquarters in D.C, confirming the first one and also granting him temporary leave with pay. It carried the name of George Ritter. His immediate boss back at the office.

He looked at Dunn and said, "How did you do this?"

Dunn smiled and said, "It really was quite easy given your years of experience with the F.B.I. and the three years of R.O.T.C. you took in high school. We, meaning the Pentagon and I, thought it would help expedite matters if you could take orders directly from me."

"I see," said Jim. "Do I have a choice in the matter?"

"Yes you do, son. But seeing as how your record shows previous applications to a military academy, without much luck I might add. And seeing as how I feel obligated to you for saving two lives aboard this ship... I thought this could be a way for me to show my appreciation. But it's strictly up to you." Dunn sat down in the Captain's chair and waited. "You can take it or leave it."

Jim thought for a moment. He keenly remembered his rejection to the Air Force Academy, and clearly this man was trying to make up for it somehow. He smiled at Captain Dunn and said, "Ah, what the hell. Where do I sign up?"

Captain Dunn was all smiles as a seaman mysteriously appeared by his side and handed Jim numerous documents for his signature. "Don't worry about your medical records; we've already received copies of those from the F.B.I.," Captain Dunn said.

The seaman showed Jim where to sign and afterwards Captain Dunn, looking at Jim, said, "Now that that's all cleared up, raise your right hand and repeat after me..."

Jim was back in his cabin after getting officer's khakis and a cap from disbursement. Along the way, a CWO had loaned him an extra pair of bars that he now pinned to his collar. He smiled when he looked in the mirror and thought how strange it was that after all these years he had finally gotten his bars after all.

He strapped the Sig Sauer pistol to his hip, put on the baseball like cap and preceded back to the bridge where he reported to Captain Dunn.

When he entered the bridge, he snapped to attention and said, "Sir, Warrant Officer Green reporting for duty, sir!" He saluted and the entire bridge broke out in cheers as Captain Dunn returned his salute and said, "Well done, sailor."

Some of the men stepped up and shook his hand. When things finally settled back down, Dunn pointed out that they were approaching the rendezvous point. He told Jim to report to Lieutenant J.G. Sparks on the lower deck where the Formula 1 was tethered. He would be going out as a member of the assault team. Jim said, "Aye aye, Captain," and hurried down to the speedboat.

Sparks, a small but rugged looking man of Greek descent, was waiting for him when he arrived and handed him a bulletproof vest and a life preserver as they boarded the Formula 1. Jim found himself in the company of four other men who all greeted him warmly as he found a seat and strapped in. They all carried weapons of some kind or another. Sparks asked if he needed a weapon.

Jim pulled out his Sig Sauer and Sparks whistled softly and said, "Well I guess that answers that question," and gave the cast off sign to a seaman on the deck of the Harpoon.

Sparks took a seat at the wheel of the speed boat and ran a quick check to make sure the engines were idling smoothly and everyone was strapped in properly. He engaged the forward lever and the Formula 1 pulled away from the Harpoon gradually picking up speed. The seas were still a little choppy from the now distant Tropical storm Sarah, and the boat jumped from one wave to another as the wind whistled by their ears. After about ten minutes, Jim, who was sitting directly behind Sparks, yelled out, "Hey, Lieutenant. Where are we headed?"

"We've discovered an anchorage about a half mile around that atoll directly ahead," Sparks yelled back. "We think that's where our boy Alvarez is waiting for one of his drops."

Jim could see the flat little island with just a few palm trees scattered here and there and realized it couldn't have been more than a mile across. As they started to go around it, he saw two boats sitting in the water on the starboard side near the atoll. As they approached, the boats began to move in the same direction as they were closing on them at the same time. Sparks yelled, "There's our Bahamian buddies right on time."

All three boats moved through water at about 30 knots and in a little lagoon just on the other side of the Island Jim could see what looked like a trawler making for the open sea.

They had been spotted and the boat was trying to make a run for it. The three speedboats quickly caught up with the trawler, surrounding it on both sides. Before they could go any further a helicopter flew overhead from behind them and hovered over the boat.

Using its loud speaker, it announced, "This is the Bahamian Navy. You are surrounded. Come out with your hands up. If you carry weapons, throw them in the water. I repeat. Come out with your hands up."

Slowly five men and two women came out from inside the trawler. Two of the men carried handguns which they promptly threw into the water. At that point assault teams from all three speed boats swarmed on board sweeping the entire boat while they cuffed and restrained the prisoners. Jim was one of the U.S. team to board the trawler with his weapon drawn. Checking the faces of all the men, he soon found the one he was looking for.

He looked at Sparks and said, "Got him."

Sparks in turn talked to a Bahamian who seemed to be in charge and pointed to Ruiz Alvarez. The Bahamian nodded once, and Alvarez was led over the side of the trawler and put in the Formula 1 with the U.S. assault team. The rest of the prisoners were put in the Bahamian boats while a few Bahamian personnel remained aboard the trawler to make the pickup as soon as it happened.

Later on, the airplane, once it had made its drop, was spotted by the helicopter and told to land in the water. Refusing to do so, it was shot down by a heat seeking missile carried by the helicopter. Otherwise the operation had gone smoothly and without incident.

The Bahamians had gotten the dope and some key members of Alvarez's drug ring and the Americans had Alvarez.

Ruiz Alvarez could not understand why he was not being taken away in the same direction as his people until they came in view of the Harpoon.

When he saw the American flag hoisted on the mainsail, Alvarez began to vehemently curse the assault team saying they had no right to do this to him. He pleaded to be turned over to the Bahamians. After all, there were many in Nassau whom he had been paying handsomely for protection. And who were more than willing to see to it that he continued to do so.

But this time there would be no deals or payoffs with the Americans. More importantly they now had the man whose information could help them coerce Castro and the Cuban's to stop their illicit drug business and bring to a halt a large part of the drug trade in the U.S.

No one paid attention to Alvarez until they got him aboard the Harpoon. He was taken and put in the ships brig under 24 hour guard. Upon returning to the Harpoon, Jim and the rest of the assault team were debriefed in the stateroom and afterwards Jim sought out Jennifer and found her in her cabin with the ever-present corpsman. She was delighted to see him and asked if he would stay with her awhile. He did and they talked for a very long time.

Returning to his cabin, he thought about getting something to eat, but decided against it. He lay down on his bunk and rolled the things Jennifer had told him over in his mind. When he finally got back to

Washington D.C. he was going to pay a visit to Mr. Perez if he was still there and find out why he would want to hurt such a sweet little girl.

On impulse he got up from his bunk and went to the sickbay. There was a corpsman on duty that greeted him as he walked in. There were only two patients in the sickbay.

Peters was there in one of the beds reading a magazine. He said hello and had a few words before wishing him well. He then walked over to the woman's bed.

She was either still unconscious or in a coma. So he sat down and looked in her face for a while before subconsciously taking her hand. And for a little while he began to feel at peace as he felt the vibrations of the Harpoon gently making its way to Miami as evening began to fall. It had been a long day.

A very long day.

CHAPTER 11

A few days earlier, three men pulled up to the Pirates Cove Marina asking the whereabouts of Captain Paul Stokes for the purpose of engaging his charter service. They were informed by the marina's manager that the Captain was on vacation in the Bahamas at the time, but there were many other experienced men and women available.

The three men declined any further assistance, instead choosing to rent a boat and head out by themselves, the manager would later recall. After a couple of days Shortwave 1, 2, and 4 tracked the Angel trough the Caribbean where they finally caught up with her off the Grand Bahamas.

They attempted to kill everyone on board and were in the process of setting the Angel on fire when one of their members spotted what looked like two speed boats and a helicopter in the distance headed their way.

They immediately left the scene as fast as they could without starting the fire so as not to draw attention to themselves.

But the Bahamian attack force was not interested in a couple of deep sea fishing boats. They were headed to one of their Island outposts to await a rendezvous with a Cuban backed drug trafficker and the U.S Coast Guard. Sometime later S 1, 2, and 4 returned to the area where they had originally found the Angel, but this time after an extensive search, they found nothing and headed back to Florida.

They arrived back in Palm Bay the next day and ransacked the house where Paul Stokes lived. Finding nothing of relevance, they went to the airport, placed a coded call to Adrian, and boarded a flight back to D.C.

Adrian sat in his living room and considered his future. It didn't take a fool to see that things were beginning to fall apart around the seams.

Pest control had called in a report from Florida that left a lot to be desired. And for some reason he hadn't heard from S3 in days. He knew the job S3 tried to do had failed. The detective who had visited him was the same one who had thwarted S3's bombing attempt. But S3 had gotten away, so the news reports said.

He must have been hurt somehow and was not yet able to reach him by phone. And if that wasn't enough, where in the world was his daughter? Pest control said she was not aboard the Angel when they took it out. Beverly, her brother, and their son John were there, but no Jennifer. It was enough to make a grown man cry.

After all his planning and hard work, it was hard to conceive of a more disastrous turn of events possibly occurring just when he was about to make his move.

He knew he would be forced to wait until these same events unraveled themselves. Because if he were to move now, it would undoubtedly point the finger of culpability at him. At the very least connecting him to the disappearance of Beverly and the kids and may be even to the death of that Private I. He thought about

Beverly and wondered if she knew it was him behind the attack before she died. After he thought about it awhile, he believed she probably did. He got up from his chair, put on a coat and left the house.

Detective Todd Morrison had been out of the hospital a few days and was home convalescing when he got a call from Rick Gates. Rick said the Captain wanted to know if he were up to investigating a cold Jane Doe, an unidentified dead female.

Todd replied, "Sure, why not." Since he wasn't really doing anything he wouldn't mind looking at some woman's dead body and trying to figure out who she was and how she got that way.

Rick laughed over the phone and told Todd he would be by to pick him up in one hour. Todd said fine and hung. He had taken a shower and was fully dressed when Rick arrived. Putting on his coat he left his house and got into an unmarked car with Rick.

Rick looked at his partner and said, "It's good to have you back, Sarge."

"Yeah, yeah, I know, just drive," Todd said. They hadn't gone far when Todd turned in his seat and said to Rick, "You know, it really is kind of nice to get back in the saddle. I mean, just sitting in that house all by myself was beginning to drive me up the wall."

Rick smiled and said, "What you need, Sarge, is a good woman to help you occupy all your free time. Now it just so happens that Mary has a friend who is single, ready, willing, and able, if you get my drift."

"Listen up Rick," Todd said with mock severity, "You and that wife of yours stay out of my business! Is that understood?"

"Sure, anything you say, but Mary said that she expects you to be at our house on Saturday for dinner.

At which time the aforementioned lady will be in attendance."

Rick looked over at Todd as he drove and continued, "I'm sorry," he said, "I did my best to keep you out of this, but you know how Mary is."

Rick sighed and said, "She just won't take no for an answer. But I tell you What, If you call Mary and tell her..."

Todd interrupted him. "Oh no," he said. "You're not getting me in trouble with that she devil. I'll be there!"

They both broke out in laughter.

When they arrived on the scene and pulled to a stop, two cruisers and a coroner's van were waiting. Todd found himself at the sight of an old abandoned warehouse just a few miles outside of D.C. but still within their jurisdiction. Todd and Rick got out of the car as a police man with two teenage boys in tow approached. Todd knew the officer and greeted him warmly. Afterwards the officer said, "These are the two boys that found the body, Sarge."

Todd asked the boys their names and to recount their story. They said they had been at the warehouse looking for scrap metal all day which they sold to a local foundry. Todd asked them didn't they know the warehouse was private property and that signs were posted all around stating that fact.

They both looked at him in amazement and replied they hadn't seen any signs anywhere and were just trying to make an honest buck.

Sarge said okay, and asked how they found the body.

They said that at some point during their search, they noticed a funny smell coming from one of the buildings. Upon investigation they found the grisly remains of the rotting corpse of a woman lying partially wrapped up in a blanket. They hurried to the nearest phone booth and called the police, just in case there was a reward.

Todd looked at them and thanked them for doing their civic duty. He turned to the policeman and asked if he had gotten their statement; he said he had and Todd turned back to the two smiling young men and told them that if they didn't get the hell out of there pronto, he would have them arrested for trespassing. They looked at him in shock and he yelled, "Now move." They took off running towards a pickup full of junk and drove away.

The policeman led Todd and Rick to the site where the body still lay. Upon inspection, they determined the body had been driven there and dumped without too much concern.

The coroner told them he believed it had been there about two weeks due to the stage of decomposition. Todd asked the coroner to get him dentals as soon as possible and without missing a beat the coroner replied he would have them at Todd's office no later than 5 p.m..

With nothing left to do, the two detectives drove to headquarters. Todd was greeted by everyone as he entered the building and made his way to his desk where he was surrounded by more friends and co-workers. The impromptu reunion was broken up by Captain Harvey who ushered Todd into his office.

He waved Todd into a seat as he sat behind his desk. "Todd," he said, "tell me what you know about this guy Adrian Perez." Todd bought the Captain up to date concerning the investigation into the death of Bill

Rhoads and his subsequent conversation with Adrian Perez.

When Todd finished, Captain Harvey said, "The Commissioner would like for you to stand off on this one."

Todd said, "What do you mean stand off? Bill Rhoads was my best friend and my heart tells me that this bastard Perez probably had something to do with his death. And now you sit there telling me to lay down and play dead?"

Captain Harvey leaned back in his chair and said, "Don't get your ass up on your shoulders. Something came up, that's all. By Monday you'll be back on the case and this time, you'll have the added help of the F.B.I.

Todd got up from his seat and said, "No way! You can tell the Commissioner that he can take my badge and stick it where the sun don't shine! No way I'm lying down on this one."

"Now Todd."

"What?" Todd exclaimed.

"Seems they found Mr. Perez's missing family. One of their agents here in D.C has been assigned to assist us in this matter, but he won't be back in to D.C at least until Thursday.

"Todd, listen," Bob said leaning forward in his seat. "We don't want to make a mistake and scare Mr. Perez off at this point, especially if he's the one behind Bill's death. And don't forget that Bill was my friend, too, and I would like to see the son of a bitch who murdered him caught just as much as you do."

Todd slowly sat back down in his seat and asked, "Where is the Perez family now?"

"I can't tell you that, though I can tell you it has something to do with National Security."

"You're kidding."

"No, that's what the F.B.I. said. By the way, we think the guy with the bomb showed up at Cedar Sinai hospital the same day as the explosion. There was an emergency room treatment of a John Doe who suffered an eye loss and severe facial damage. But unfortunately some time that night he disappeared after being treated and put unconscious in a room. That's about all I can tell you. But we'll get him, I know we will."

Captain Harvey stood up and stretched out his hand to his friend. They shook hands and Todd left the office without another word and returned to his desk. He took his seat and called Rick on the intercom and asked if he wanted to go get lunch. Rick agreed and they both went out together.

When they got back Todd saw a message on his desk that said to call someone named Joey Mastrano. He dialed the number and when a man answered Todd stated who he was. The person on the other end identified himself as being Joey Mastrano, one of the two teenagers who found the dead woman's body.

He told Todd they had found something else when they discovered the body but had forgotten to mention it to the police at the time.

He wanted to know if he could stop by and drop it off. Todd said sure and gave him the address before hanging up. Joey Mastrano was pissed off as he left home in his pickup. His friend Terry refused to come to the police station with him and return the pocketbook they had found earlier with the dead woman. There was almost two hundred dollars in it and at first they had argued whether to keep it or not. Finally they decided to turn it in out of fear that someone might figure out they had it in their possession. And now he was on his way there by himself.

When he reached the police station he double parked and went inside giving the pocketbook to the officer at the front desk and telling him who it was for before scurrying back to his pickup truck and disappearing into the afternoon traffic.

Todd was sitting at his desk when one of the rookies bought the pocketbook to him. He called Rick on the intercom and they both analyzed the contents of the pocketbook extensively.

At some point Todd picked up the phone and called the Cuban Consul asking if they had a Lisa Alvarez working there and was told that they did. He asked if she was there and was then told that she was on leave but would be back any day. Todd replied that he seriously doubted that and asked to speak to whoever her boss was. The person at the other end replied that would be the Chief Attaché, Adrian Perez. But unfortunately he also was away and unavailable at that time.

Todd thanked the person, hung up and stared at the ceiling. Rick looked at him inquisitively.

The contents of the handbag had contained a piece of explosive evidence. Todd picked up the Cuban Consul photo I.D. of Lisa Alvarez, and he began to get angry with every passing moment believing that there could be no doubt Adrian Perez was likely to be behind this mess, too. He began to wonder what it was that Bill Rhoads had uncovered about the man. Whatever it was had most certainly cost him his life, and he told

Rick to call the photo lab and see if they had developed any of the film discovered in a hidden drawer of the desk in Bill Rhoads office.

If they had, he said, he wanted it right away. After Rick made the call, Todd told him about his conversation with the Cuban Consul and who Lisa Alvarez worked for. Rick whistled softly and said, "What do you think, Sarge? Is this guy the black plague or what?"

"Yea," Todd said, "seems like everything he touches turns up dead. I wonder who's next?" When Todd spoke those words a chill ran up his spine. He began to wish the guy from the F.B.I. would hurry up and get there before it was too late. Because he had an awful feeling that he knew exactly who would be next.

And by the look in Rick's eyes Todd knew that he had guessed who it would be, too. Detective Sgt. Todd Morrison.

The dental prints and related reports on Jane Doe that arrived later on that day from the coroner's office would eventually substantiate what Todd and Rick had already determined. Jane Doe was in reality a Cuban national named Lisa Alvarez, who had been stabbed to death and unceremoniously dumped at an abandoned warehouse outside of town.

It was a pitiful way to meet the maker, and as much as Todd wanted to proceed he knew that the Captain had been right on the money. This was no time to do something that might tip Adrian Perez off and send him running for cover. Until the F.B.I. agent arrived on Thursday he would take the next week off and try to enjoy himself.

When they left the office that evening, Todd broke from his normal routine and went shopping. He wanted to be ready for his blind date at Rick's on Saturday and somewhat surprised at himself, he wanted to look his best. After all, what if?

S3 was sick. He lay in bed in agonizing pain, deliriously drifting in and out of consciousness and at times he imagined he was still a member of the Baden-Meinhoff terrorist gang in Stuttgart Germany and in German, talked to members of his old cell. During these spells, he didn't realize all of his old friends were dead and gone and that he was the only one who had survived that final terrible assault on October 3, 1979, by slipping away to Brazil the day before German authorities tracked down and killed the entire group.

There were those who believed his survival was proof of collaboration with the authorities and that he had been the one who revealed the locations of all the hiding places of the Baden-Meinhoff gang.

This could not have been further from the truth, though for years he was outcast from the underground terrorist community because of this belief. Then he met Adrian Perez.

It had come to his attention via a few remaining acquaintances he still had in the underground, that Adrian was looking for someone of his abilities and was willing to pay well.

For S3 it was a new lease on life. He would be able to perform the same duties he had been trained so well for and at the same time regain a certain amount of self value. So to Adrian he gave his loyalty and in return he received a new home in America.

On the fourth day S3 awoke from the spells for the last time and though he didn't know it then, he would later realize he was about to undergo an amazing metamorphosis. As he made his way to the bathroom and looked in the mirror, what he saw there made him want to look away, but in fascination he gazed at the caricature of his old self reflecting back at him. His blood streaked face was swollen to almost twice its normal size and his nose and left cheek had somehow been molded into one large ball of flesh.

When he removed the bandage he'd received at the hospital from around the left side of his face and head, his left eye socket was a dark and brooding void that seemed to have no bottom, looking in the mirror and it scared the shit out of him.

He didn't want to get lost in that void and desperately struggled to hold on to reality, but to no avail. S3 grabbed on to the bathroom sink and screamed, "No! No! Nooo" In a great rage he screamed again, "I need some freaking sympathy..." and sank, crying to the bathroom floor, rolled up into a whimpering ball and sucked his thumb. His metamorphosis was now complete and irreversible.

Later on, he got up and removed all his blood- and vomit-covered clothes and after taking a handful of pain killers, he washed the right side of his face, (he would never touch the left side again) running a tub of hot bath water and cleansed the rest of his body. He donned some clean clothes and went down to the basement where he kept his armament.

S3 removed an old fashion German luger from behind the wall which he strapped under his arm and put two full clips in his jacket pocket before leaving the basement. Taking a fresh overcoat from the hallway closet and putting it on, he left the house, walked to the nearest Metro entrance where he boarded the Red Line headed for midtown D.C., and took a seat at the rear of the first passenger cars amidst numerous stares in his direction.

At the third stop, a group of six skinheads dressed in leather jackets, jeans, and combat boots got on the same car as S3 and walked towards the rear intimidating passengers as they went.

Seeing S3 sitting there, one of the leaders, who wore a black leather jacket painted all over with skulls and cross bones, pointed in S3's direction and laughed aloud saying, "GODDAMN! Look at this Ugly Mother."

The rest of the skinheads gathered around S3 waving their fists, as the leader said, "What the hell you doing on my train? I can't allow anybody as ugly as you on my train. So get the hell off, you one eyed geek."

S3 looked at the man's jacket and had a most clever idea. He stood up as if he were going to leave but instead turned to the leader and in his thick guttural German accent said, "May I please have your jacket?" He looked straight at the leader with a smile on his face and continued, "I really do need it, you see. It is most important that you give it to me." In S3's demented state of mind the deadhead designs painted on the jacket were communicating with him and they wanted to be friends. Voices in S3's head were telling him to take the jacket. They wanted to be his friend and the only way to do so was for S3 to wear the jacket.

It would be good to have friends again, it had been so long. Again he insisted to the man, "Give me the jacket please."

The leader looked at S3 in amazement, and then a look of hatred crossed his face. He stepped back and pulled a long knife from the instep of one of his combat boots thrusting it up to S3's face. "You want my jacket? Try and take it you Quasimodo bastard."

In a lightening move, S3 grabbed the skinhead's wrist in his left hand and the knife hand in his right, snapping back with tremendous force and breaking the wrist all in one swift action. The skinhead yelled in pain and his companions all reacted, reaching for concealed weapons.

Still holding the man, S3 kicked him in the groin viciously and slammed his right elbow into his temple as he fell to the floor, causing multiple blood vessel ruptures that would eventually kill the man.

Unbeknownst to S3, a black man called Hollywood, who saw the fight start from his seat at the front of the metro car, bent down behind the seat in front of him and tried to call 911 on his cell, but it wouldn't work in the tunnel. But he was able to wave and get the attention of the driver in his cubicle across the aisle from him causing him to look back at the melee at the other end of the car.

S3 leaned on his right foot and side kicked the face of one of the other skinheads who attempted to close in on him, breaking his jaw and knocking him unconscious. The rest of the group stepped back in order to marshal their forces into one quick rush, but by then S3 had drawn the German Luger.

The skinheads made the mistake of standing there wondering what to do next and S3 indiscriminately shot at the heads of two more of their group, killing them instantly.

All the passengers on the train screamed and tried crawled under their seats to find cover except for Hollywood who tried to keep his eyes on all the action and could hear the driver's screaming for help on the train's radio transmitter.

When one of the two remaining skinheads tried to run away down the aisle, S3 leaped towards him shooting him twice in the back sending him sprawling over three people crouched on the floor of the moving train. The dead man wound up laying in front of Hollywood, and he squeezed further back behind the seats.

S3 turned to the remaining skinhead and instructed him to remove the jacket from his fallen companion's body.

The man did as he was instructed and handed it to S3, who took off his own two coats and transferred the two bullet clips to the pocket of his new jacket and put the luger back in the holster under his arm. With solemn reverence, he put on the deadhead jacket as the train pulled into the next stop.

He thanked the remaining skinhead for being so helpful during such a trying time and walked to the double doors as the incredulous young man sat down among his fallen companions and put his shaking head into his hands. S3 stood by the double doors, laughing and talking to all his new jacket friends as the train came to stop. When the doors opened, he walked by the people waiting to board the train and disappeared into the mulling crowd of the station, chatting merrily away. The metro police were running down the escalator trying to find the source of the trouble. S3 bound up the steps on the opposite side, never seeing the police as he walked away, talking to his new friends in the jacket.

Hollywood remained on the train a few minutes assessing all the carnage, glad to be alive. He didn't wait for the cops to show up before he, too, left hurriedly. He had done all he could do. After all, junkies and cops tended to not get along. Hollywood side stepped the police ask they rushed the train car.

CHAPTER 12

Coast Guard Cutter Harpoon

Tuesday evening, the Harpoon was approximately 200 miles southeast of Miami in International waters and making about 15 knots into a head wind.

She would reach her final destination the following morning where F.B.I. agents would be waiting to take Ruiz Alvarez into custody and fly him back to D.C.

And though onboard ship, the officers and crew went about performing their regular duties pursuant to routine operations, there was a noticeable degree of excitement in the air. Earlier that day, Beverly Perez had finally awoken from her long deep sleep and everyone aboard the Harpoon felt a warm sense of pride.

With their help, she had survived almost certain death and once again was able to hold her daughter in her arms even though she would never again see her son alive. She had accepted the news of John and Paul's death with understanding and finality, because she remembered well the men and the deadly gunfire that nearly killed her, also. Her physical recovery was nothing less than a miracle.

The ship had a surgeon flown in on a helicopter, and the doctor had performed two superb surgical operations, removing a bullet lodged against her skull and extracting another one from her side.

A third bullet had passed through her right arm, but left a clean exit wound, easily repaired. All in all she had been very lucky and over the past two days her body had helped itself so much in the healing process, that when she did awaken she was able to sit up and ask for something to drink. The first person she saw when she awoke was an officer who was sitting by her bed. He got up and poured her some water from a pitcher sitting on a small table next to her bed and handed her the cup.

She drank deeply, draining the cup and asked for some more. As she drank the second cup, she asked the officer where she was and if he was a doctor.

He smiled and said she was on a U.S. Coast Guard vessel headed for Miami and he was not the doctor, but it was time that she saw him. He left in a hurry and spoke to a corpsman who called the doctor on the phone. In a few minutes the doctor entered the sickbay and asked her how she was feeling.

She said very well and wanted to know how she got there. He said the Captain would be down shortly and would explain everything.

When the Captain arrived shortly thereafter, Jennifer was with him. Seeing her mother sitting up in bed, she broke out in a huge smile and shouted, "Mom."

She ran to her mother leaping in her arms and they both cried and talked for some time until the Captain sat down in a chair beside the bed. Beverly wrenched in pain from Jennifer's jump. Jennifer immediately understood that the Captain and her mother needed time to talk together so she wiped her eyes and told her mother she was going to find Jim and tell him the good news. She rushed out of the sickbay in search of her friend.

Beverly asked the Captain who Jim was, and he replied that he would let her know that all in good time.

But first he needed her to tell him everything she could remember about what happened on the Angel and even before and afterwards he would fill in the rest of the story.

In the back of the sickbay, a seaman sat down and quietly started typing on a stenograph machine.

When Captain Dunn returned to the bridge, he had the record of their conversation faxed to the Pentagon, who in turn relayed a copy to the F.B.I. That same night Captain Dunn handed Jim Green a new set of orders via the ships telex, giving him specific directions concerning Beverly and Jennifer Perez and Ruiz Alvarez.

That same telex ordered him to fly back to Washington immediately upon arrival in Miami and report to a Captain Harvey at the D.C. Police to await further instructions. He couldn't believe it.

Ruiz Alvarez was the biggest collar of his career and now they were taking it away from him at the very end and it didn't make sense.

He'd been putting off going to visit Beverly Perez all evening and decided that maybe this would be a good time, if she was still awake.

He went to the sickbay and found Beverly eating from a tray of food while talking to one of the corpsmen, and when she saw Jim come in she handed the tray to the corpsman and straightened out her bed covers. The corpsman smiled and walked away as Jim sat in the chair next to the bed. Beverly spoke first, "So, you're the famous Jim Green."

"How did you know that?" Jim said aloud, and Beverly laughed.

"Why, between my daughter and just about everyone else on this ship describing you to me, I would have recognized you in a room with the lights out from all their descriptions."

Jim smiled not quite sure what to say.

"I really don't know how to thank you for saving my daughter's life. Everyone on this ship has done so much for us, but Jennifer seems to think that you're her guardian angel.

"And as any mother would be able to tell, she has grown extremely attached to you and it will be difficult to reconcile this fact when the time comes." Her face softened as she continued. "The corpsmen tell me that you were here most of time I was unconscious." She lowered her head and said, "I don't know why. But somehow I know it made a difference, and I'm grateful for that, too."

She lifted her face and gave Jim a smile that made his heart feel like a breezy spring day. This woman that he hardly knew was becoming very special to him, and he knew that he was going to do everything in his power to find a way to be a part of her and Jennifer's life.

He reached out and took her hand in his and was rewarded with a gentle squeeze. They began the process of understanding each other by talking into the early morning hours, She kept dozing off and coming to, until she finally tired and fell asleep. Then and only then did he leave her side to return to his own cabin.

The next morning Jim was awakened by the ships call to reveille. He got up and showered, putting on his old clothes afterwards before returning the officer's khakis to disbursement.

He was mildly surprised when they informed him that the khakis were now a part of his belongings.

As an officer returning to inactive status, he might be recalled to duty someday and would be out of uniform without them. He returned to his cabin and packed the khakis away in one of his bags.

At breakfast he saw the CWO who had given him the officer's bars and offered to return them, but was politely told to keep them, also. He had a light breakfast and went to the sickbay to see how Beverly was doing, finding both Captain Dunn and Jennifer there with her as he came in.

She looked at him and smiled.

The captain said, "Well Jim, you and these two wonderful ladies will be leaving us today I'm sorry to say." He stuck out his hand and Jim shook it.

"It's been a pleasure, sir," Jim said.

"Seriously, son," Dunn said, "if you ever get tired of those people over at the F.B.I., you can activate your commission at any time."

Jim said, "So it was really on the level."

"Sure was and is! Come visit me sometime will you, Jim?"

They shook hands one more time before Captain Dunn said his well wishes to Beverly and Jennifer and left the sickbay.

Jim turned to Beverly. She looked at him and said, "I've been told that we're to be taken into protective custody soon. "

"Yes." Jim answered.

"Captain Dunn's been ordered to turn you over to F.B.I. agents waiting in Miami. We are beginning to believe that the attempt made on your lives was not accidental and may be linked somehow to a spy network or something of that sort, so for your own protection, you will be transported to a safe house somewhere where all your needs will be looked after.

"Needless to say, as you yourself have communicated to us, we also believe that your husband, Adrian Perez, is undoubtedly involved in this thing."

Jennifer sat down on the bed by her mother and they held each other's hand. Jennifer unwittingly echoed her mother's thoughts when she asked, "Will you be coming with us, Jim?"

"No. I've been ordered back to Washington, but if it's all right, I'd like to check up on you from time to time. And someday soon after this is all over, well..." He paused but Beverly finished for him.

"Yes, Jim, that would be nice."

But Jennifer didn't think it was safe for Jim to leave them yet and voiced her opinion. "But if you go who's going to watch out for us?" She began to cry. No matter how much they tried to comfort her, Jennifer would have none of it, and eventually Jim said he had to go and saying goodbye he left them in the sickbay together.

He returned to his cabin, retrieved his bags and made his way out on deck where he found most of the crew standing at parade rest as the ship pulled into Miami harbor.

Ruiz Alvarez was also on deck, in hand and foot cuffs, shouldered by two seamen carrying automatic weapons in their hands.

When the ship docked and the gangplank was extended down to the pier, everyone returned to their duties.

Jim turned to the officer on watch and asked permission to leave the ship, walking down the gangplank to the ground where he was met by a number of fellow F.B.I. agents who shook his hand and congratulated him on a good collar. He turned around and looked up just as Alvarez was being led down the gangplank.

When they reached the bottom, the agents exchanged glances before Alvarez was taken by F.B.I. agents and pushed into the rear of a black van with a red light on top. The vehicle took off to the sound of sirens led by three cars in front and followed by the same number of cars at the rear.

Jim got into a car that was waiting for him and breathed a sigh of relief as it, too, pulled away from the Harpoon.

No matter what, Ruiz Alvarez was now in custody, which meant he had done the job he had been assigned to do and nothing and no one could ever change that. He had some time to think about Beverly and Jennifer and knew they would be well taken care of until the day when the fates brought them back together again.

He hoped that it wouldn't be too long before he saw them again as the car made its way through the morning traffic to the airport. Having been cleared by airport security with a special code, the car was driven out to the tarmac where his plane stood by with the engines running.

He boarded the plane and handed his bags to a stewardess who showed him to a first class seat. He ordered the first of three beers for the long flight back to D.C.

When the plane landed in D.C., Jim went to his apartment and changed into some clean clothes before going to D.C. police headquarters. When he got there he met with Captain Bob Harvey who filled him in on all the current events to date and the reason why he was there in the first place.

Bill Rhoads, before he died had spoken to a number of people implicating Adrian Perez in a Cuban spy operation, which of course was F.B.I. business as Jim already knew, but Perez was also under suspicion in several homicide cases including the murder of Bill Rhodes.

So the powers that be in their infinite wisdom had decided that Jim would be assigned to assist the police in this matter and affect an F.B.I. presence for the duration of the investigations.

Jim expressed his hope that his presence could lend assistance to the police. Captain Harvey told him to take the rest of the day off and report back tomorrow when he would meet the officer in charge of the Perez investigations.

They shook hands, and Jim left the building headed for Georgetown to a jazz club he knew of and spent the rest of the night unwinding and listening to the music.

In another part of town, Adrian Perez was sitting at the dining room table having dinner when the phone rang. He got up, went into the kitchen and answered it. At the other end he heard S3's voice.

"This is Shortwave 3. There is static. I repeat, there is static. I've got it all over me. I repeat. I got shit sticking all over me, *Mein Fuhrer. Befehl, mein fuhrer ich beten.*"

There was a long pause, and S3 said, "*Entschuldigen sie, es tut mir leid. Viel gluck Mein Fuhrer. Auf Wiedersehen.*" and hung up at the other end.

Adrian slowly put the phone on its hook. He wasn't sure of everything S3 said. But he understood enough German to know that S3 needed him and was asking for direction. But there was nothing he could do. Everyone in pest control understood that. There could be no exceptions. If you screwed up, you were on your own.

Over the past few days the news services reported that the police were still on the lookout for a one-eyed man who shot and killed a number of people on the subway a few days earlier and the same man was now wanted in connection with a bomb explosion that occurred almost two weeks ago. The police were also asking for the eye witness that the conductor had seen leave the train right after the murders. No. There was nothing he could do.

Wait!

What was it... Something that he said...

Something about shit sticking all over him. S3 was no longer himself, he knew, but like his father use to say, "No es bueno pensar en lo pasada." It is not good to think of what is past.

With that thought in mind, Adrian went back into the dining room and finished his dinner.

He decided that it was almost time for him to depart. So for the rest of the night Adrian Perez carefully packed those things which he felt would be most important on his coming journey.

He also made calls to Zurich and transferred funds through a network of accounts that he had spent years setting up and carefully maintaining in preparation for this very moment. He was ready.

The next morning, Jim Green, Todd Morrison and Rick Gates formally shook hands and sat down in Captain Harvey's office down at D.C. Central Precinct.

The first thing Captain Harvey did was to distribute copies of the recently developed film found in Bill Rhoads office.

The pictures showed people going in and out of an apartment and also copies of National Security Agency documents which were clearly stamped classified. Captain Harvey said, "Gentlemen, for national security reasons, these documents will not leave this office, though you have all been cleared to look them over. As you can see, Mr. Adrian Perez has been a very busy man. The apartment you see in the pictures before you no longer exists; it was fire bombed a couple of days ago. And a real nasty fire it was. It killed two children and a babysitter who got trapped inside the complex.

"Any ideas as to who the woman might be?"

Todd Morrison stiffened in his seat. "Captain," he said, "I'm sure this is Perez's secretary, Lisa Alvarez."

"That's right, Todd. But, since the apartment doesn't belong... Excuse me... didn't belong to Perez, I meant to say, we can't officially tie him to the document or the murder of Lisa Alvarez as of yet. But what we can do is make things pretty hot for him by bringing him in on suspicion in the murder of Bill Rhoads based on the pictures and the testimony of Beverly Perez.

"Now if I can have those pictures, please, you fellows can go get Mr. Perez and escort him back here to one of our holding cells, and see if that don't shake his tree a bit. Here's the warrant for his arrest." And he handed it to Todd.

Rick Gates, looking more than a little perplexed, stood up and said, "Excuse me, Captain, but you seem to have forgotten about something."

"What's that Detective Gates?"

"Diplomatic immunity," Rick said.

Captain Harvey looked at Rick and said, "Agent Green would you mind explaining the Federal Government's position in this case?"

Jim said, "In 1960, due to a failed coup attempt on Fidel Castro's government called the Bay of Pigs, all diplomatic ties between the U.S. and Cuba were severed by Castro. And even though they now maintain a Consul here in D.C. they will not recognize diplomatic immunity for any Cuban national formally charged with murder or the violation of the Secrets Act."

"Very good, Mr. Green." spoke the Captain

"Are there any more questions, Mr. Gates?"

Rick muttered, "No sir."

"Then what are you waiting for? A goddamn embroidered invitation? Go get him."

Todd and Jim had a good laugh at Rick's expense as they left the office and continued to break out in fits of laughter all the way to the home of Adrian Perez, while Rick brooded in the backseat of the car.

Todd and Jim went to the front door and knocked, calling out Adrian's name. While Rick remained by the car. Todd tried the door knob and the door swung open. Todd searched the downstairs and Jim went upstairs. Outside, Rick decided to check around the rear of the house. And as he walked along a side fence, he came to a detached garage and turned around to look up at the back of the house.

Out of the corner of his eye he saw a blurred movement to his rear and wheeled to see, standing just ahead of him was a visage unlike anything he had ever seen before. He froze in his tracks, too paralyzed to reach for his gun and it cost him his life. Inside the house Jim and Todd heard two shots fired from the outside.

They rushed out the front door and ran to the back where they found Rick lying on the ground. He had been shot once in the heart and once in the head and it didn't take them long to realize he was gone.

And so was Adrian Perez.

SHORTWAVE: PART TWO

CHAPTER 13

The Flight

Adrian Perez sat comfortably in his first class seat aboard Virgin Airlines L 1011 bound for London, England. He was traveling under the name and cover of Roberto Diaz, wealthy business man from La Paz, Bolivia. The night before, he had driven to New York City to catch this particular flight. He felt no remorse or sadness about leaving his previous life and true identity behind in D.C.

"*No es bueno pensar en lo pasada.*" *Oh well, all's well that ends well.* It was a smooth flight all the way across the Atlantic, and Adrian felt all the tensions, relaxing for the first time in weeks.

He was able to enjoy the amenities of first class like dining on Cordon Bleu with creamed carrots and rice which he helped go down with a half bottle of Brut champagne.

During the flight he struck up a conversation with one of the stewardesses and arranged to meet her at her hotel later that evening once they reached London. His old charm was still a force to be reckoned with, and he laughed to himself.

When they landed at Heathrow he promised to call the stewardess as soon as he got situated and disembarked the plane. There was one nervous moment when one of the British customs officials questioned him at length about what he would be doing in England during his stay. He said he would be in the country at least three months looking at building sites for his new chain of health spas.

Then there was some discrepancy about the lack of a visa for someone who intended to stay in the country for such an extended visit.

The customs official told him he would have to get a visa from the Bolivian Embassy if he wanted to remain in England for more than two months. And with typical British charm, he smiled at Adrian handing him back his false passport and told him to enjoy his stay.

Adrian had no sooner left customs than a chauffeur holding up a card with his new name on it was waiting to pick him up. The man took his bags and escorted him to a Rolls Royce Silver Spur limousine. After the chauffeur put his bags in the trunk, Adrian instructed him to wait. In a few minutes he espied the stewardess he had met on the flight leaving the airport with two of the other crew. He waved her over to the car and offered to give her and her companions a ride to their hotel. After some discussion they accepted his offer and getting their baggage in the trunk, also, they all got into the limousine where bottles of wine and champagne were chilling on ice.

On the ride to London, Adrian found that the girls had a two-week layover.

So he decided to put off the plastic surgery until they were gone. And the next two weeks were a whirlwind of fun and pleasure.

His suite at the Ritz Carlton became the launching pad for whatever they wanted to do, whether it was dining, dancing, gambling, or nights out on the town, a good time was had by all.

Adrian eventually made love to two of the woman, but that never seemed to get in the way of their *triumvirate*.

Adrian became known at various establishments as Roberto the Great. The man with not one, not two, but three beautiful ladies. A reputation he himself helped to foster. He seemed to have unlimited funds and was regarded in the same manner as the oil rich Arab Sheiks around London. The special attention paid him made Adrian feel important beyond his wildest dreams. But he was also smart enough to know that until he had the operation, he was in danger of being recognized by any of the world police agencies who one day would undoubtedly come looking for him.

The girls finally left amid tearful good byes and promises of a reunion. But Adrian had no such intentions.

He got rid of the limousine and checked out of the Ritz, opting for a flat over a garment shop on one of the busiest streets in the world, Carnaby Street. He moved in during the night so as not to be seen and made sure those first few days that if he went outside, his face was covered with a scarf.

In his flat above the famed shopping district, he would spend the next six weeks mostly hidden from the world outside while undergoing a radical transformation.

In another part of the city, called Chelsea, was the private clinic of a Maxillary Facial Specialist who would perform the plastic surgery.

And every so often with the exception of the first week, he would travel by cab back and forth to the clinic for whatever treatment was necessary. He and the doctor spent hours initially looking at pictures of different face types and even took pictures of his own to re-draw until they both decided on a look that was pleasing and at the same time, totally different from the way he actually looked.

He spent the first week recovering from the bone restructuring done during the first procedure, sedated in a private hospital by the Thames River.

From his bed side window he could see the Tower of London looming in the distance and in his drugged state, fearfully wondered if they caught him, would that tower be the place of his retribution.

Casually asking about it one day, one of the nurses told him that it was no longer used for such purposes. But you could take a tour of the tower and hear stories about frightful things that once went on there.

He felt greatly relieved at the revelation and decided he would take the tour as soon as he was well enough. Maybe along with the same nurse who had told him about it. The doctor and owner of the clinic had come highly recommended by members of the same underground network where he had recruited most of pest control.

Though the clinic's facilities could not be called state of the art by any means, it was the anonymity afforded the clients that really mattered. No names were ever used at any time from the very first contact on to the last.

Only numbers were used to identify patients and the doctor and his staff knew how to keep their mouths closed, especially since some of their clients were among the who's who of the terrorist world and would not tolerate disclosure. There were no wagging tongues here.

As weeks of inactivity followed, he passed the time watching the BBC television broadcasts in his flat and on the second day of the fifth week, he saw something that galvanized him into action.

There on the TV looking back at him was his old self, Adrian Perez, the Cuban diplomat. It was during one of those Interpol programs that were becoming so popular in London just like "America's Most Wanted."

A couple of old pictures and a description of him was shown, but what surprised him most were the number of crimes he was now credited with.

They had somehow been able to tie him to all that "Wet" business back in the U.S. with the exception of the firebombing of his old apartment in D.C. and the deaths resulting therein.

But the Canadian express train wreck, the bombing, police shootings at the Rhoads office building, the murder of his wife and kids, and even the death of Detective Rick Gates, (which came as a surprise as it was something he knew nothing about) were now being attributed to him.

Yes. Someone had figured it all out in less time that he thought possible. With perverse fascination he watched as he was described as a mass murderer and ruthless leader of a deadly spy network that stopped at nothing to serve its own purpose.

Mass murderer. He kind of liked the ring of it, and he would not be averse to more murder and mayhem if need be, right now he was faced with a new problem.

He had to move again and into a deeper hole this time until the bandages on his face could finally come off.

Over the next few days he created a new cover for himself and arranged to take a room in a small hotel in Greenrow Brixton.

He was now known as Victor Romero, a Puerto Rican landowner, who had been severely burned in the face as result of a car accident.

He moved from Carnaby Street to Brixton in the dead of night in the off chance that someone noticed his movements during the day.

If London was the melting pot of the world, then Brixton was a black cover on the pot.

In the midst of the African and Jamaican communities, he would be able to lose himself. No one would ask questions of a man with a bandaged face sporting a little money around in the right places.

The people of Brixton had a long history of economic and racial strife and they were not on good terms with British authorities. So they were closed mouthed about what went on in their small but close-knit community. Since money was always in short demand there, and Adrian was able to capitalize upon the situation.

A few days after he arrived at Manner Arms, the rundown establishment where he'd acquired a room, he quietly went about making himself invaluable to the people of Greenrow.

After some investigation on his part, he started by contributing a 1000 pounds to the local children's care center where there was a shortage of food because of Parliament cutbacks. The donation was supposed to remain anonymous, but Adrian made sure he let it slip, his identity, by mailing that cashier's check with the help of the woman behind the front desk at Manner Arms.

At first people said the rumor of a car accident (which he himself propagated) pointed to the likelihood that all was not right with Mr. Romero.

In any event, insisted the skeptics, why would someone as wealthy as he was want to come and live in Greenrow?

But on the other hand, those who were directly affected by his gifts countered by saying that someone who had been in such a disfiguring accident would not want to be around the well-to-do and might even have been outcast by his own people. And so it continued, Adrian giving his gifts and people thinking he was a little crazy.

Then one day, two weeks after his arrival in Greenrow, the local church went up in a fire. A fire, under the cover of night, that Adrian set himself, that totally destroyed the church, after burning through the night in spite of the best efforts of the numerous fire companies that responded to the blaze.

The effect on the community was devastating. The church had served as a beacon, drawing all the different racial groups and political factions together under one roof.

The day after the fire was extinguished, almost everyone in Greenrow gathered outside of the rubble from the aftermath of the fire that still smoldered and hissed in a bone chilling rain, where the church used to stand. To see what, if anything, could be done to rebuild such an important cornerstone of the community.

The meeting was opened with a prayer from the church pastor and afterwards the matter of what to do was open to discussion. Suggestions began rolling back and forth through the crowd of people gathered there, but in a poor community it is difficult to rebuild that which takes a life time to create in the first place. The day wore on as a feeling of growing despair surfaced throughout the crowd.

It seemed that all possible avenues and considerations had been explored and rejected due to economic concerns.

When it seemed like the crowd was about to disperse in defeat, it was then that Adrian made his single most important contribution to his cause of secrecy. He walked to the front of the crowd and lifting his arms in the air said, "Good people of Greenrow... Now I know you don't know me, and I don't know you, but it seems to me that what you need here are the proper materials to rebuild this most beloved shrine."

Someone in the crowd said, "That's right, mate, but who's to give them to us? Certainly not a crazy bloke as yourself." Some of those in the crowd broke out in laughter, but others shouted to let him speak.

Adrian continued, "Well you're right, sir, I can't give it all to you, but what I can do is help you get started." He reached inside his coat pocket and removed an envelope saying, "What I have here is a cashier's check for ten thousand pounds. This should be enough to buy the materials necessary to start a foundation and frame work for a new church. Some of you men out there are masons and carpenters and together should be able to do the initial construction. Am I right?"

An excited murmur rippled through the crowd. Here was the preverbal light at the end of the tunnel. Talk of bake sales and fund raisers to raise more needed funds began to take precedent.

Adrian handed the check to the pastor to thunderous applause and made his way through the crowd amidst many slaps on the back and shouts of gratitude and thanks.

For the next six months Adrian (or Mr. Romero as he was now known) had the blessings and protection of the community at large. He let it be known that his presence there was to remain anonymous and the people of Greenrow were more than willing to oblige him.

He was safe from the prying eyes of the outside world for the time being, but he soon met and romanced a young Jamaican woman named Etti Samms who became his lover and occasional companion. When she became pregnant he made promises of marriage which he would never keep. Because soon after that his bandages would came off.

That day, the doctor, after some observation pronounced the operation a great success.

Adrian couldn't agree more. When he looked in the mirror the doctor handed him, he was astonished to see a face he had never seen before.

He could see through the dark blue swellings that still remained, a face of undetermined origin about 35 to 40 years of age, that would be very handsome in due time. The old Adrian Perez truly no longer existed, and in a couple of weeks, he had his picture taken and sent off to his contact in the underground that made fake passports.

He still kept his bandages on in public. And one day returning from a visit with Etti, he was told that there was a package in the mail slot for him. He took it and hurried upstairs to his room.

This was the moment he had carefully planned for over the past three years.

He immediately packed his few belongings and left the hotel where he had spent the past six months telling the proprietor that he'd made arrangements to move into an apartment with Etti.

The woman wished the two of them much luck and he walked out the door of the Manor Arms, caught a cab and directed the driver to take him to Gatwick Airport. At the airport, he went to the men's room and removed the bandages from his face, and using his new passport, he caught a plane leaving England for the last time.

The people of Greenrow would wonder at the disappearance of Victor Romero for years to come, and Etti Samms would search in vain for him throughout London until long after the baby was born.

She named him Victor and loved him very much. Once he was old enough to understand, she told him that his father was lost in an airplane crash. No one in Greenrow ever told him any different. Adrian Perez, Roberto Diaz, and now Victor Romero no longer existed.

The funeral of Rick Gates had been a particularly sad affair.

Todd Morrison was deeply affected by the· death of his partner and took it very hard. He and Mary Gates stood shoulder to shoulder at the grave site trying their best to support each other.

For Todd it was the loss of his second best friend in as many months and for Mary it was the loss a good husband and father to her children.

Todd vowed that as long as he had a breath to breathe, Mary and the kids would not want for anything. He was prepared to dedicate his life to their well-being and he let Mary know it.

She was grateful and said for Todd not to worry about them. She was sure that in a little while she and the children would be just fine.

But Todd knew better. Rick had not been a rich man and did not leave any family behind as he was the only child of parents who had both died when he was still just a child. So he made sure as time went by that Mary and the kids were all right and if at any time they needed anything, he was always there to help.

Quietly, Mary appreciated Todd's help and they became like brother and sister. The two little girls were always delighted to see him whenever he came to visit, and Mary became his confidant in matters of work and the heart. Whenever there was new flame in his life, if she didn't meet with Mary's approval, the relationship was quietly terminated. And if something were bothering him about work, it was Mary who helped him keep a cool head about it.

Then Mary met a fellow at work and started dating him, with Todd's approval, and eventually they fell in love and got married. Todd was the best man, and it was one of the most cherished moments of his life. He knew that Rick would have approved of the young man Mary had chosen and was proud to be known as Uncle Todd. At the reception, he was seated in a place of honor as a very important member of Mary's family. It was, in contrast to the funeral, a very happy occasion.

Also during this time the hunt for Adrian Perez had taken a turn for the better. Rightly guessing that he'd probably left the country, the F.B.I. issued a worldwide alert for the apprehension and capture of the fugitive, and Interpol picked up his trail in London. One of the stewardesses who had partied with Adrian saw Interpol's program and recognized the man she knew as Roberto Diaz.

She called the number for Interpol written down at the end of the program and reported the incident to them.

As a result of her call, all three of the stewardesses were eventually brought in for questioning, and pretty soon Interpol agents had a very good pitcher of Adrian's first couple of weeks in the UK. They quickly started asking questions around London for any information that could help them in their search for the missing man.

The trail led them to numerous nightclubs and restaurants, and everyone they showed his picture to remember him as the great Roberto.

The man had not one, not two, but three beautiful women. Investigators were perplexed as to why Perez would risk being seen by so many people, until the trail turned cold, and it seemed as if Adrian Perez had once again disappeared. His trail was as cold as a frozen tundra.

It would be a long time before they would once more pick up his trail. The U.S. authorities turned their attention to an unknown assailant described by many witnesses as a middle-aged man with a horribly deformed face, who was a suspect in the deaths of numerous people during an altercation on a Washington, D.C. public train.

The same person had also been witnessed in the vicinity of the Perez house the same day Rick Gates was murder.

After his phone call to Perez, S3's jacket friends, voices told him how unfair it was for Perez to treat them that way after all he'd done for him. He was the one who did all the nasty little jobs Perez was too weak to do himself. Wasn't that wonderful bombing of the Canadian Express proof of his undying loyalty?

They were angry! They wouldn't stand by and watch him degraded anymore, and together they stole a car and drove to within a few blocks of Adrian's house. Making his way to the rear of the house, S3 arrived just in time to see three plainclothes detectives pull up and two of them walked up the walkway to the front door/ S3 almost shouted with glee.

One of the men was the same detective who'd been the cause of all his misery and he'd been meaning to find out all about him. Seeing him there was a miracle and cannot have worked out any better.

He quietly hid behind the garage to see if they would bring Adrian out under arrest. If they did, the plan developed by the newly appointed leader of the jacket people, was to sneak up behind them and shoot all three men. S3 liked the voices who's new leader who he called Hans. It was nice having someone else do all the thinking, and Hans was just the deadhead for the job.

While he waited, he noticed one of detectives had decided to explore around the house. S3 cursed under his breath, and Hans told him to be cool and let Christopher Columbus make his great discovery. When the detective got to the rear of the house he turned around to look up at the second-floor windows.

S3 snuck out from behind the garage with his gun drawn. The officer must have noticed him because he spun around to face S3 and froze. Winking his good eye S3 said, "Welcome to America" and shot the detective once in the heart and then in the head.

Detective Rick Gates fell dead to the ground, and S3 ran back behind the garage and down a side street making his way to the stolen car. He got in and drove forty miles to the Baltimore Aquarium and Marina where he finally parked at a restaurant.

Going inside, he waited to be seated by a hostess who, upon seeing the man, nearly fainted with fright, but nonetheless showed him to a seat.

Other patrons in the restaurant were appalled at him, worried that they had to eat in the company of such a grotesque looking person who obviously hadn't bathed in weeks, and reeked from a disgustingly vile odor which emanated throughout the entire room.

In reality the left side of his face had become a mass of pus filled sores, and it was the infection that the patrons could smell. A number of the people closest to him got up and left while others tried not to notice him.

S3 picked up the menu and asked Hans what he thought they should all have.

Hans told him to order a raw steak, and S3 felt a chill run down his back, wondering why he didn't think of that. He called for a waitress and most of the ones on the floor scurried into the kitchen before the hostess could pick one of them.

One unlucky girl, who had been inside the restroom when S3 arrived, was sent to the table. Her head down, she reached for the receipt book in her pocket, and upon reaching his table she raised her head and said, "May I take, Uh, Can I... Oh, I... your order please?"

S3 looked directly at the girl and smiled, saying, "We would like one uncooked steak *freulein* and a pitcher of beer. *Bitte*."

She backed away and once out of range covered her mouth with her hand, running back into the restroom, locking the door behind her and repeatedly throwing up in the toilet.

After a while the hostess went to see if she was okay, and the girl shouted to her behind the locked door, "I am not coming back out and wait on that... that... thing."

The hostess pleaded and then became stern, saying, "You have a job to do. Now open the door right this minute!"

The girl screamed, "TAKE YOUR F-ING JOB AND STICK IT UP YOUR SKINNY ASS!! I AIN'T COMING OUT."

In desperation, the hostess went back to the kitchen area in hopes of getting another waitress, but most of the girls, seeing her head that way, grabbed their coats in a desperate rush to get out of the place. Eventually the hostess reluctantly retook his order

Once he was finally served, S3 decided that raw meat was the most delicious food in the world. All the other deadheads agreed. He savored the flesh in his mouth and slobbered the beer down directly from the pitcher burping with sheer pleasure. His taste buds would never again be satisfied with cooked meat which he now considered beneath him. And if raw beef tasted so good...

When he finished his meal he left the payment by the cash register since there was no longer anyone left in the restaurant to give it to. He left the place with the new and strange craving inside of him. Hans said it was part of his coming transformation.

So he got back in the car, driving it to a quiet street in D.C. before abandoning it, walking back to his abode in deep conversation with Hans.

CHAPTER 14

The F.B.I., based on the documents Bill Rhoads uncovered before his death, began surveillance of a number of people at the National Security Agency suspected of secreting classified documents of U.S. activities in Cuba to Adrian Perez or Hector Gomez. Six arrests were subsequently made, and those who stood trial were found guilty of espionage and given substantial prison sentences.

Hector Gomez tried to flee back to Cuba but was caught entering Canada, and a few months later he was extradited back to the U.S. where he stood trial as a spy in a District Federal Court of Washington, D.C.

The media had a field day. It was the first time a Cuban diplomat had stood trial in the U.S. for spying. And even though the Cuban government filed a complaint with the U.N., the trial proceeded nonetheless.

One interested party in the whole matter was Ruiz Alvarez. As he sat in his maximum security cell at Leavenworth, having already been tried and convicted of drug trafficking, he followed the proceedings in the papers with increasing alarm. His sister, Lisa, worked for Adrian Perez who was also being charged in this particular case and in spite of a massive worldwide manhunt, was yet to be captured.

He had reason to be worried. Eventually Lisa became sought after by the prosecution as a witness, and the D.C. police were forced to make her murder a matter of public record. Ruiz was devastated. He knew it could only have been Adrian Perez who ordered the death of his sister.

She had told him about their stormy affair on many occasions, and there was no doubt in his mind that Perez probably got rid of her because of what she knew about him.

Lisa often told him that Perez wanted to marry her and bragged how very soon he was going to make her a rich woman. That she was willing to give up her position with Cuban intelligence to run away this man spoke to Ruiz in volumes, enough to realize that Perez was certain to have a lot of money hidden away somewhere.

And for Ruiz Alvarez it was easy to put one and one together and come up with where and how Perez managed to make this money. To this end Ruiz was special among the hundreds of dealers who had made pacts with Cuba via Perez to pay money for the right to use Cuban soil.

He himself was Cuban, and it was his sister Lisa who put him in contact with Perez. If she said Perez had a lot of money, there was no doubt that he did. And in Ruiz's mind there was only one way he could have gotten it.

Jim Green woke up in a sweat. He'd just had another dream like the ones he'd been getting lately. In these dreams Jennifer Perez was, once again, in some kind of trouble, though this time he couldn't remember precisely what it was. In any event he decided that it was time to pay Jennifer and Beverly a visit. He was pleasantly surprised at how much he missed them, and the thought of seeing them again made him smile.

He looked at the clock on the bed stand. It read 5:45 am. He figured he might as well get up and headed for the shower. As he bathed he thought about the Perez case and how the fugitive seemed to have vanished from sight somewhere in England, if he was still in England. They'd lost his trail in London and for months now no other leads had turned up.

It was doubly hard on Todd Morrison, he knew, and thought about calling the big man for breakfast but decided against it.

He decided to get on the horn right away and check in with the duty officer at F.B.I. Central in case anything might have come in concerning Perez. There wasn't much likelihood of a new lead, but since he was up, he might as well call and see. London was six hours ahead and it would be in the middle of the work day there.

When he called he found out nothing new about Perez, but there was a massage for him to contact the F.B.I. Office in Leavenworth, Kansas.

At 7 am Jim went to the sporting club downtown and worked out on the stair master for an hour before showering and walking to his office two blocks away. There he went to the cafeteria and had breakfast. Afterwards, withdrawing to his office, he sat down at his desk, turned on the computer and went through his electronic mail. He had to be over at Todd's office early that day, so he made his call to Leavenworth a quick one.

He was told by the agent who answered that Ruiz Alvarez had requested a meeting with the F.B.I., and him in particular, concerning a possible deal based on information he was sure they could use about Adrian Perez.

Jim thanked the agent at the other end and hung up.

He hurried over to Todd's office, told him about Alvarez's request, and they decided to make the trip to Leavenworth together. Captain Harvey wasn't there that day so they bucked the request on up to the major who gave them the go ahead.

Jim called his boss at the F.B.I. and got permission to requisition the necessary round trip tickets and hotel reservations. By noon they were on a plane headed to Kansas.

Ruiz Alvarez waited at a table in the law hall of Leavenworth prison. The law hall was a special room full of law books, where prisoners could get information about the law and how it could be used in their behalf.

As Ruiz waited for the two law officers to arrive, he contemplated his future. He was looking at 15 to 20 with no hope of an early parole, and that was hard time by anyone's standard. He had to get out somehow, if just to seek revenge on the man who had murdered his sister. Lisa had been a beautiful woman who knew how to take care of herself, and Ruiz was sure that the only way whoever murdered her could have got the drop was with the help of Perez. Otherwise she would have been too dangerous to approach. Of this he was sure.

As a child growing up in Cuba, Ruiz had often played soccer with the other boys and much to his and their chagrin; Lisa would join in their games and was almost unstoppable.

She could best any boy her size in a fight and often beat him to the punch if she had to. When she was recruited into the army she learned many things that made her deadly in a fight, and she had the brains to see that her future was best served in the intelligence branches. They readily accepted her.

Ruiz came to the U.S. at the age of twenty, but that didn't stop him from becoming one of the fastest rising drug dealers in the country.

Lisa always knew about her brother's criminal activities but never divulged this secret to anyone other than Adrian. In fact she often helped him with information and was the one who came up with the idea for him to pose as a man called Hector Ramus in order to disguise his comings and goings.

When she introduced him to Adrian Perez he immediately disliked the man and often argued with Lisa about her relationship with someone who was married with children. He felt that with this one man, she had left herself vulnerable, and there was nothing he could do to make her see the heartbreak she could have been letting herself in for.

Ruiz clinched his fist together in realization that he had been way off the mark as far as what Adrian was capable of doing to her. *Breaking her heart was not what had been in his mind. But murder? Yes. Murder was what the man had intended all along. What else?* Ruiz banged his fists down on the table in anguish. *If I just could have made her listen she would still be alive. Maybe.*

The door opened at the other end of the law hall, and Jim and Todd walked in with Ruiz's lawyer. The three men took seats at the table, and Ruiz eyed them as his lawyer said, "Gentlemen, my client has information that he feels is of great importance to your investigation of one, Mr. Adrian Perez."

Ruiz looked at Jim thinking here was the man responsible for his downfall.

But Jim as always was enigmatic.

Even during his trial, Ruiz could never fathom what he was thinking as he sat in the courtroom until the final verdict was read and even then he seemed to show no emotion. He gave Ruiz the jitters then as he did now.

"Furthermore," the lawyer continued, "we feel that this information is valuable enough to warrant reconsideration of my client's sentence and the prospect of an early parole."

Jim was the first to answer. "Well, as you both well know, we're not empowered to make that kind of a deal, but we'll be glad to pass it on to whoever is if the information is worth the bother."

Alvarez jumped out of his seat before his lawyer could stop him and shouted, "Worth the bother? Worth the bother? What do you mean, worth the bother? The *marichon* killed my sister! And you talk about worth the bother?" Ruiz's lawyer was trying to get him to calm down by pulling on his arm. Ruiz said, "Man take your hand off of me or you're goin' draw back a stump in another second!"

The lawyer released his arm, and Ruiz sat back down, fuming. "Ah gentlemen," the lawyer said, "you must understand that my client has only been recently made aware of the death of his only sister and being behind bars, well as you can see he's been under a lot stress and rightly so, l might add."

Todd spoke for the first time; "Mr. Alvarez, what makes you think Perez killed your sister?"

Ruiz still fuming said, "She was his lover and on top of that, she worked for the bastard and that's why he killed her. She knew too much."

Todd closed his eyes. It finally hit home that Lisa Alvarez and Ruiz Alvarez were brother and sister. Jim still hadn't figured it out and looked at Todd wondering if he was feeling sick or something. He heard Todd whisper the name Lisa Alvarez and then he too realized it.

The sheer shock of the coincidence was almost too great. Jim shakily said maybe it would be best to stop the proceedings until the following day when a court stenographer could be present to take Ruiz's testimony.

He also assured them that he would personally put in a good word for Ruiz once they had gotten his affidavit. They got up and left, neither one saying anything to the other until they reached the hotel.

Together they went to Jim's room. Jim called the local F.B.I. to make sure there would be a stenographer at the prison the following day. Then he called Washington to see what kind of deal he could get for Alvarez while putting in a good word for him just as he said he would.

Jim knew they were playing a game of tag, and Alvarez was it. If they could get a solid lead from the information they got from him. Jim was given the green light to offer a reduced sentence. The Alvarez case had been an important conviction for the Bureau, but catching Adrian Perez had far more consequences.

The following day the two men returned to the prison and questioned Alvarez at length. They were able to find out that Perez had been receiving money from Alvarez and other drug dealers and funneling it back to Cuba.

Alvarez also related that he was sure that Perez was skimming off the top and probably had a sizable amount hidden away somewhere.

He said, "If you follow the money it will lead you to him. Just follow the money." Todd asked Ruiz to explain just how they should go about it. Ruiz said he didn't really know but in any event that finding the money was probably the only way to smoke him out.

Jim asked Ruiz how much money he had paid to Perez and the lawyer interrupted and said it would be in the best interest of his client not to answer that question.

Jim wanted to know if Ruiz had had any dealings with Hector Gomez. Ruiz said he never saw the man before seeing him on T.V. but Lisa often spoke about him. Jim wanted to know what she had to say. Ruiz commented "Well I know that Lisa considered him a milk toast even though he was the boss and that it was Perez who really ran the show at the Consul in Washington. At least that is what Lisa told me. She used to say that if it weren't for Adrian that old school teacher would have been returned back to Cuba years ago."

Jim asked if he knew anything about the transmission of classified documents back to Cuba and if so who was involved.

The lawyer refused to allow Ruiz to answer that question also. Jim had a feeling that Ruiz knew more about the Perez-Gomez spy network but at that time chose not to make an issue of it. Ruiz didn't know what it meant to be squeezed yet, and there would come a day when Mr. Alvarez would gladly give all the information he had or thought he had. But first things first.

After the questioning had finished, Jim told Ruiz and his lawyer that he had been authorized to tell them that if his information was good, Ruiz would get a reduced sentence of five to ten with a possibility of parole in three.

He would have to be transferred to a federal prison near Washington D.C. for easy access, just in case the Bureau needed to clarify any parts of his testimony.

After some consultation, both Ruiz and his lawyer agreed.

Jim and Todd shook hands with the two men, left the prison, and went back to their hotel where they checked out and caught the next flight back to D.C.

As soon as they returned to Todd's office, Captain Harvey was waiting for them and ushered them into his office. Pointing to a seat, he turned to Todd and said, "What the hell do you mean by going over my head like that Detective Morrison? I'm still in charge of this goddamn office, and you'd better not forget that again!" The two men shifted uneasily in their seats as he continued. "This is my goddamn precinct and I'll be damned if I'm going to allow anyone to usurp my authority here, and that goes for the goddamn F.B.I., too," he shouted looking in Jim's direction.

"Now the both of you can get the hell out of my office."

"But Bob..." Todd tried to interpose.

Captain Harvey literally screamed, "I said get the hell out of my office!" Both men got to their feet and were just about to go when the Captain said," By the way, Mr. Green, your services will no longer be required. I will see to it that you are reassigned to your own office at the Bureau. Goodbye!"

The two men looked at each other and went back to Todd's desk. "Whew! I wonder what's got into him?" Jim asked.

Todd threw his hands up in the air. "Lord only knows," he said, as baffled as Jim was. "Well, I guess we might as well go have a drink or two," Todd said to Jim.

They put on their coats and went around the corner to a bar that Todd knew of and remained there for the rest of the evening.

The next morning Jim returned to his office at the F.B.I. His boss wanted to know what had happened, and Jim readily assessed him of the events leading up to his termination of the assignment with the police.

Jim also indicated his feelings of confusion in the affair since he felt sure he had done nothing wrong. At that point he indicated to his boss the desire to visit with Beverly and Jennifer Perez and was given a few days leave to do so. They were now living at a safe house in Connecticut, and if he wanted to get there before dark he had to hurry.

He left the Bureau for his apartment and repacked his overnight bag with clean clothes before calling Todd Morrison to tell him where he would be in case something came up, and he needed his help. He then hung up and rushed to the airport, just making the next shuttle to New Haven.

Detective Todd Morrison was grateful for the phone call from Jim. He really liked the man and valued his judgment. He could tell that Jim held him in high regard also and he wished they could have remained associates throughout the duration of the Perez case.

He didn't know why he had taken such a dim view of Bob Harvey's decision to split them up, but he did.

And it didn't make matters any better that he and the Captain were such old acquaintances. As he left his office he was deep in thought and would not have been able to see the man watching him as he walked down the sidewalk anyway.

The man was cloaked behind the glass of a car so darkly tinted, it was almost impossible to see through to the interior. The car was parked along the sidewalk and when Todd was far enough away it pulled off and followed him at a safe distance.

Upon reaching the corner, Todd decided not to pick up his car across the intersection at the police parking lot but to take a detour and go by the same bar he and Jim had gone to the day before. When he turned the corner down the street to where the bar was, the car following him, pulling to a stop as the man inside watched him disappear inside the bar.

After some thought as to what he should do next, the driver decided there was no rush, or there would be other days and other chances. He pulled away into the growing rush hour traffic.

A few hours later Jim Green arrived at New Haven Airport where he was again met by local agents. They took him to the safe house where the Perez's were being kept, arriving just after dark. The door was opened by a female agent who ushered them inside. She was both house keeper and guard for the two females and had been with them since their arrival. The two agents who'd met Jim at the airport disappeared to some unknown place in the house while Jim stood in the foyer.

Presently, both Beverly and Jennifer came from the direction of the rear of the house to greet him. Jennifer ran to him and jumped into his arms. She cried. "Oh Jim, I've missed you so much, and I never thought you were going to come see me."

She felt good in Jim's arms and he squeezed her tightly before releasing her, saying, "Well, I missed you too, Jen, and I'm really glad to see that you're looking so well!" He turned his attention to Beverly Perez. "I'm glad to see that you are also doing very well, Beverly."

He put his hand out to her, but she ignored it and walked up to him, gently kissing him on the cheek. He turned a little red in the face though not without being noticed by Jennifer who jumped up and down laughing as she whooped and exclaimed, "Mommy made Jim blush! Mommy made Jim blush!" If anything, after that Jim's face turned even redder.

Beverly laughed and said, "Don't worry, Jennifer's just so excited to see you again that's all. She really has missed you an awful lot, and this is an unexpected pleasure for her." With a soft look in her eyes, she said, "And for me, too."

She told Jennifer to go and ask Donna if she would fix something cold to drink, and Jennifer skipped away calling Donnas' name.

Beverly took Jim's hand in hers and guided him into the living room where they sat down and began to discuss what had transpired since they last saw each other.

The day they left the Harpoon, Beverly had been taken to the local naval hospital where she was kept under observation until it was determined that she was fit to travel, and then she, along with her daughter, was transferred to the house in which they now resided. Jennifer was enrolled in a school just a few blocks away and had adjusted very quickly.

Though lately she had started having bad dreams about something, which she found increasingly difficult to talk about. Beverly asked Jim if maybe he would have a talk with her about it because she couldn't get any more out of about it. He said that he'd wondered if she were having dreams and it was one of the reasons he had come to see them. He related the experience that both he and Jennifer shared while he was aboard the Harpoon, and she was aboard the Angel.

He felt sure it was something that could not be explained away as being mere coincidence. Not only that, but he was also beginning to have strange and disturbing dreams himself. And again they concerned Jennifer.

Beverly looked at Jim and knew that this man would not lie to her. He had to be taken seriously, and she asked what possibly could be done. Jim said that he wasn't sure, but fortunately their present status in the witness protection program would continue until Adrian was finally caught and put away. He related there was one more thing he wanted to do and that was to see if he couldn't get assigned temporarily to the New Haven office.

That way he could be around just in case there was some merit to the dreams he and Jennifer were having.

Beverly would not say it out loud, but she hoped with all her heart that he would be able to either stay with them or come back one day soon. Jennifer returned with Donna who carried a tray with three cups and a pitcher of lemonade on it and sat it on a low table in front of the sofa. There was a sense of security all around, and as Jim got to know Donna, he was confident that she was an able bodied agent, more than capable of taking care of her charges.

Talking with her, Jim learned there were three agents on duty in the house at all times and two exchange agents sat in unmarked cars parked in front and at the rear of the house twenty-four hours a day.

The agency figured if Adrian Perez was capable of causing the death of hundreds of people on a train in order to eliminate his family, then he certainly wouldn't think twice about trying it again if he thought for one minute they were still alive.

After a while Jim decided to have a talk with Jennifer. They put on their coats and went outside together and sat down on the porch in the March air as Jim nodded to the agent across the street in the unmarked car.

"Jennifer," he said, holding her hand in his. "Is there anything you want to talk about? Anything that might be bothering you?"

She seemed to tense for a minute and seeming to think for a while she asked, "Are you having anymore dreams like before?"

He replied, "Yes."

She relaxed and told him about the dreams she kept having about a man who was chasing her, and no matter how she tried she just couldn't seem to get away.

He asked, "Can you remember what this man looks like in your dreams? Is it someone you know or maybe have seen before?"

Jennifer was quiet and sat for a long time in deep concentration before answering. "I can't see him yet. It's like he's still far away, but I know he's coming."

"Do you think he can see you?"

"No, at least I don't think so. Not yet anyway."

She looked at the ground and again was quiet for a while, and then she said, "Jim?"

"What is it, Jen?"

"There's something else."

"What?" he asked.

"Well it's only happened a couple of times, but I dreamed there was another man who was chasing you and someone with you."

Jim laughed nervously and said, "Well let him come if he wants to. I'll be waiting."

"But I can see this man in my dreams."

He swallowed "You can... Well... what does he look like?"

She started to cry, "Oh Jim," she said, "I'm so scared." He put his arm around her and tried to be of some comfort.

"He's so horrible! It's like... like he's that horrible monster I used to read about when I was still a little girl."

He smiled at what she said, thinking how much of a little girl she still was.

He shook his head and asked, "What monster could frighten a big girl like you now?" He questioned teasingly.

She wiped her eyes and admonished him by saying, "You really should get serious." As she got up and walked back to the door.

"Wait, Jennifer." Jim said, "I'm sorry. I didn't mean to tease you. Please tell me about this other man who's after me."

She reached for the door and opened it, turning just before going in to say; "He's not a man, at least not anymore he isn't. He's the Cyclops. That's what he is now, the Cyclops."

She turned and went inside the house shutting the door behind her. Jim sat on the steps for a while longer and looked up at the sky. A chill pass through his bones, and he tried to warm himself by folding his arms together, but it really didn't seem to help.

When he returned to the warmth inside the house it was a long time before the chill ultimately left his body only to be replaced with a new and more chilling fear.

Jim stayed at a nearby motel that night and visited one more day with Beverly and Jennifer. Jennifer seemed to have forgiven him for teasing her the previous night, and they had a nice time together early in the day. But as the time for his departure drew nearer, everyone's demeanor seemed to become bleaker.

Saying goodbye was the last thing on anyone's mind. To Beverly and Jennifer, Jim was someone who had gone through a bad time in their lives with them and it was hard to put into words just what he meant to them both. Jim finally said goodbye to them that evening and caught the last shuttle back to D.C.

When he got back to the apartment, he found a message on his answering machine from Todd Morrison asking him to give him a call as soon as possible. He dialed Todd's number and Todd answered. He told Jim there was something he needed to discuss with him and said he wanted it to be at a place where they could meet and not draw undue attention. Jim suggested the grass mall in front of the Aerospace Smithsonian in one hour and Todd agreed.

When Jim got there he found Todd sitting on a bench across from the Air and Space Museum. He sat down beside Todd and waited for the man to speak his mind.

The museum had been closed since earlier that evening but numerous people still walked up and down the sidewalks on both sides of the mall. Todd at last spoke up. "How was your trip to New Haven?"

"Fine, just fine"

"Did you learn anything you didn't already know?"

"Well now that you mention it, the girl told me something that could be relevant."

"What's that?"

"She's been seeing a one eyed man coming after me, and probably you, in her dreams." Jim was quiet after that and wondered what the man would make of it.

"That's one uncanny little girl."

I've been getting the feeling that someone's been watching me the past couple of days and I wouldn't be surprised if it's the one eyed man."

The both looked around into the darkness before Todd continued. "A policeman who's been showing a sketch made from eyewitness accounts of the one-eyed man who shot the skinheads on the train, bought me the address of a possible suspect. It seems there's this one-eyed guy the neighbors on his beat seem to think is pretty weird. From what the officer says, he could be our man."

"Have you informed Captain Harvey?"

"Not yet."

"What are you waiting for?"

"I don't know, I just don't know."

"Have you told anyone, Todd?" Jim asked.

"I've told you," he replied as he closely watched the people walking through the mall.

Jim took a deep breath and speculated about how much warmer the weather was here in D.C. in contrast to New Haven, Connecticut.

He thought about Beverly and Jennifer and wondered what they were doing right now and if they were okay.

Suddenly Todd stood up and looking down at Jim said, "Well, I think I'll pay this guy a visit. You want to come along?"

"I wouldn't miss it for the world," quipped Jim.

CHAPTER 15

When Captain Harvey received the phone call, he was in bed. He picked up the receiver and listened for a moment before giving a reply. He hung up, got out of the bed thinking how much he'd been dreading the possibility of that particular phone call for a long time now and it was with much trepidation that he dressed to go meet the caller.

Bob Harvey considered himself a good man, and as a police officer he'd always done things by the book. But there had been one instance earlier in his career, when faced with a serious financial problem, he hadn't done things by the book.

And he felt he'd been paying for it ever since. At that time he was approached by a man who needed someone put away and was willing to pay the then Sergeant Harvey a lot of money to do it. It seemed at the time to be the answer to a crisis he was going through. His wife had finally gotten fed up with the long hours he had to spend on the job in order to move up through the ranks, just because he was not one of those college trained officers and the ensuing divorce had left him virtually homeless and penniless.

It seemed so unfair that the same system that he'd worked so hard for would turn its head while he was being displaced, and he felt abandoned by both his wife and the system at large.

So he accepted the money and did the job. It was just a matter of falsifying certain records he had access to so that a certain man would wind up in prison for a long time. And his disposition at the time was the man was a known drug trafficker, and Bob had most likely done society a favor by putting him away.

But as time wore on, he was called upon to do other things, and it was getting more and more difficult to keep out of harm's way in the situation. Tonight S3 had called him to inform him of a meeting with Adrian Perez and he had to go, but this time he would put an end to things if he got the chance.

He didn't know how Adrian had managed to return to the U.S., but if he got the chance tonight, he would get the fugitive away from the others and kill him. That would effectively scatter the rest of pest control, and he'd have the distinction of doing away with a man responsible for so much death and destruction.

No one would ever find out that he was a member of Adrian's group, effectively known as Shortwave and was responsible for misleading investigators in the case although he believed that Morrison and Green were beginning to get too close. When he found out about their visit to Ruiz Alvarez he almost lost it but felt he had slowed them down for the time being.

He took out his regulation 38, made sure it was loaded and left his house, heading out into the night. The meeting place was an old deserted Masonic Temple in south Washington where many abandoned houses seemed to dominate.

Captain Harvey noted how cold it seemed to be that night as he entered through the front of the building. Once inside he found himself in a huge old foyer where candles were lit on a large table by a wall, dimly revealing dust everywhere he looked.

He called out the code phrase of recognition. "This is Shortwave 5 on the air." He waited a moment and repeated the phase. "This is Shortwave 5 on the air." He heard a voice coming from one of the other rooms.

"This is Shortwave 3 signing on."

"This is Shortwave 3 signing off. This is Dead Head 1 signing on."

What the hell is going on, Harvey wondered as he walked towards the voice. He was just reaching for his gun when S3 stepped out in front of him from one of the side rooms and hit him on the skull with an iron poker he had found somewhere inside the old building.

Captain Harvey fell to his knees not quite unconscious and S3 reached inside Harvey's coat and took the man's gun putting it in his own back pocket.

S3 lifted Harvey under the arms and dragged him down a long hallway to an open door that led down a long flight of steps. He stood the groggy man up on his feet and shoved him face forward down the steps. Harvey fell all the way down to the bottom puncturing one of his lungs, breaking his jaw and left leg on the way.

The searing pain brought him fully back to consciousness. He moaned in pain in the darkness, and hearing footsteps on the stairs, he moved around on his back to see S3 coming down towards him carrying a lit candle.

At the sight of S3's face Harvey cried out in fear. The man was hideous. The left side of his face had almost rotted away to reveal the bone underneath covered with bits and pieces of flesh. The left eye socket was totally empty of any remains, and where there had once been a nose there was now only a scarred trench running down to his lips.

As he came down the steps S3 spoke, "Hans says to tell you, you should not be afraid. He says to tell you that everything will be all right."

As he reached the bottom he pushed Harvey over on his stomach with his foot and Harvey screamed out at the shooting pain in his ribs. S3 tied his hands behind his back with wire.

Harvey croaked, "What are you doing? Where is Adrian?"

S3 said, "He will not be coming this evening."

Harvey felt a deep fear crawling under his skin which seemed to take control of his nervous system, and he started shaking uncontrollably and was afraid he might soil his pants. Then he had an idea. An idea that held a glimmer of hope, and he seized upon it.

"Where is Hans, S3? Please let me speak to Hans."

"Okay. Go ahead, he's listening."

Harvey looked around but couldn't see much through the dim .light provided by the candle. "Hans, listen to me. I don't know if Adrian has anything to do with this, but I can do for you what I did for him. I'm a police Captain, and there are a lot of things I can do to help you."

S3 retorted, "Hans says there is a lot you're going to do tonight, so don't worry because it's my graduation."

Harvey was confused but knew he had little choice but to go along with the man if he were to get out of this situation somehow. His leg was beginning to hurt unendurably, and he would have to get medical attention soon. So he tried to humor S3 by saying, "Okay. Congratulations. What exactly is it that you are graduating from."

S3 hissed. "The human race!'"

S3 stood over Harvey and with a knife cut the pants away from his body and then gouged out a large chunk of flesh from the buttocks and walked away into the darkness.

Harvey's reaction was delayed. Finally he choked out a scream of pain and shock and yelled, "Oh my God! No! Please God, help me! Help me! Please!

Harvey continued to scream until after a while he comprehended that God would not save him and began to whimper instead when his bowels discharged into the remnants of his pants mixing in with the small pool of blood that had started to form between his legs.

Somewhere in the dark he could hear S3 eating and smacking his lips, and he knew that this thing that had once been a man would almost certainly be back for more. Much more.

When Jim Green and Todd Morrison arrived at S3's house they approached cautiously with their guns drawn. The door was standing wide open as they entered to find the place cluttered with trash, but empty of any furniture. Downstairs they discovered where the arsenal was kept and found more than two suitcases full of plastic explosives, enough to take out half a block, sitting on the floor attached to a timer and set to go off at 8 am.

About the time when there would be plenty of people and cars in the street outside so the bomb would explode with maximum effect.

Todd went to the house next door and after rousing the people inside, he called the bomb disposal unit and went door to door in an effort to evacuate the block.

He and Jim withdrew to a safe distance from the house and waited for the bomb squad to come. Todd also called Captain Harvey, but not finding him home, he left a message on his answering machine informing him of the situation instead. He didn't know it then, but it was a message that Harvey would never receive.

Shortly the bomb squad arrived along with numerous fire trucks followed by some of the city's top brass who had come to assess the dilemma for themselves. Todd and Jim reported the events leading up to their discovery to the police Commissioner who had also showed up on the scene. After listening to what they had to say, he looked steadily at Todd and claimed he must have a second sense about showing up where there was a bomb involved.

He commended the men on the expeditious manner in which they handled themselves and told them that he would look into Captain Harvey's unusual behavior in the Alvarez matter. He also said that he would personally see to it the first thing in the morning that agent Green was reassigned by the F.B.I. back to the case that Captain Harvey fired him from.

The bomb squad was able to remove the timing device from the explosive and an all-points bulletin was put out for the capture of a Franz Zimmerman who had been the occupant of the house and was believed to have suffered the loss of his left eye during a shootout with the police.

Late that same night, Jennifer Perez woke up from a terrible nightmare and no matter how hard her mother tried to comfort her, she would not go back to sleep again until she knew that her friend Jim was all right.

Donna, who lived in the house with the Perezs', was able to reach Jim at his home early the next morning. Only after talking to him did Jennifer finally go back to sleep, and this time she slept peacefully.

The next day Jim was again on the Perez case with the D.C. police. It was then that he and Todd decided to see what they could do about tracking down Perez's alleged fortune.

They checked banks all over the city during the following week in what turned out to be a futile effort to make a connection, but that didn't deter them from continuing in their endeavor. Both Todd and Jim had learned a long time ago that it took long and tedious hours of often mind numbing investigation that got results.

The puzzling disappearance of Captain Harvey would normally have been a major distraction, but both men, considered the possibility the Captain might be involved and redoubled their efforts.

Jim called Beverly and asked her if she could possibly think of anything concerning Adrian's financial holdings that could be of help in their investigations, but she had already told the F.B.I. everything she could remember.

They turned their attention back to Ruiz Alvarez who was now being kept at a minimum security called Allenwood. They went to the prison and informed

Alvarez they needed more information from him with respect to Adrian's money.

Alvarez said he didn't know anything else. They didn't believe him and said his deal would be in peril if he didn't reveal whatever else he knew. Ruiz became angry and answered he already had a deal and that they couldn't do this to him.

But then suddenly he broke down and said, "Okay. Okay. I'm doing this not for you, but for my sister, God rest her soul," He gave them the first real break of the investigation.

He told them that one time Adrian could not make a money drop with him due to some unforeseen business but instructed him to deposit his payment at Barclays International Bank in D.C. and had given him the account number which he had long since thrown away, and that was everything he knew.

The two men hurried back to D.C. to follow up this new lead, but quickly learned that without the account number it was impossible to track the money down. They went back to Adrian's house and searched around with no luck.

Todd remembered the pictures Bill Rhoads had taken at the same apartment that Captain Harvey had showed them and they decided to take another look.

It had been three weeks since the disappearance of Captain Harvey and his office had in the interim been sealed by internal affairs.

They were the ones investigating his dubious departure and they had to get permission from both Internal Affairs and the Justice Department in order to get his office opened up.

Since the developed pictures contained photos of secured documents, an assistant director of the F.B.I.

was present when the office was opened and almost everyone in the building had come to take a look during this strange occasion. Even the Commissioner was there.

A member of I A broke the seal and everyone with a need to know entered the room. The officer from I A conducted the search and soon found the packet of pictures in the Captain's desk. After few moments of looking at the photos they saw a dark looking picture of a bank book. The cover was barely visible, but the name on it was still discernible. It read, "Zurich-Kloten Bahnhofstrasse!"

Todd and Jim looked at each other and smiled. Todd turned to the Commissioner and said, "Sir, I think that a trip to Switzerland is in order at this time."

The Commissioner acknowledged by saying, "I'll contact Interpol tonight and send out the necessary clearances for you men to leave right away." After further searches revealed nothing more of any real value, the office was resealed. It was clear to everyone now that Captain Harvey had withheld important information and was unquestionably involved with Perez somehow.

After everyone had left, Todd and Jim gave each other a high five and left themselves to get ready for their trip.

The next night S1 received a call to meet with the rest of Pest Control, Adrian's old group at an old deserted Masonic Temple on the south side of town. He closed up his bar early telling his patrons that his wife was sick and disappeared into the night. The bar would never open again.

CHAPTER 16

It was a typical warm spring day in Zurich as the sun reflected off the spire of St. Peter's Church and the boats that plied their trade in excursions on Lake Zurich and up the Ummat River. As Jim and Todd entered the ancient Zurich-Kroten bank they were accompanied by a local Interpol agent named Peter Klammer whom they'd met upon their arrival in the city.

Inside the bank they were introduced to one of the account executives who ushered them into a palatial conference chamber where the walls of the room were decorated with frescos, presumably commissioned by Charlemagne.

They all sat down at a large oval table where Todd and Jim presented the case of Adrian Perez to the executive. Afterwards he went to a computer sitting on a small table in the room and five minutes later returned to the oval table with a long printout.

He told them that a Cuban National named Adrian Perez did have an account with their bank but that according to Swiss law the account could only be accessed by the use of a secret account number or Mr. Perez himself. But in the case of death or extended disappearance by the signatoree on any account, the closest legal heirs could inherit the account through the Swiss courts.

Jim and Todd thanked the gentleman and told him they would return as soon as possible. They left the bank and walked back to their hotel where they had checked in earlier near the bank on Bahnhofstrasse, one of the great shopping streets in the world.

Jim made a long distance call to New Haven and the next day which happened to be a Friday. Beverly Perez arrived in Zurich.

Since the banks would be closed until Monday, Todd spent the weekend with Peter getting to know the sights while Jim and Beverly got to know each other.

Earlier that week the U.S. Department of Justice, in agreement with Interpol decided it was impossible to prove that the money in Adrian's Swiss bank account was drug-related. The decision was to turn it over to his wife and child.

The following Monday hearing was initiated with the help of Swiss banking officials, who were more than glad to relieve themselves of the stigma of protecting the interests of a mass murderer, and Beverly Perez, under the direction of the U.S. government, pleading the case of rightful inheritance before a six-member cantonal court.

After two days of testimony by banking officials, Interpol, Todd and Jim respectively, the court retired to adjudicate the case.

It was two more days before the decision and the three Americans decided to enjoy the pleasure of the city, being led around by Todd who now consider himself a seasoned traveler of Zürich and promptly had them lost on the first day out.

They all had a good laugh and enjoyed themselves immensely afterwards. Jim and Beverly's blossoming love affair came into full bloom those days in Zürich and they both agreed that no matter what happened they no longer wanted to be apart.

Todd was happy for both of them and became a little poignant and was withdrawn. When asked what was wrong, he simply stated that he was happy for them while silently making a promise to himself to look at that little lady Mary Gates, who Lucas recently introduced him to.

When the court was called back into session no one knew what to expect. As Beverly stood before the bar, the senior judge read the decision, five to one in Beverly's favor.

The only dissenting vote was by an older judge who still adhered to the protectionist philosophies of a time that was swiftly passing away.

The decision meant that one day soon, there would be no place for people like Adrian Perez to hide ill-gotten gains in Zürich, or any other place else for that matter.

It was a great victory for the forces of good in the world and they celebrated that night with Peter and the other members of Interpol.

The next day as they waited in the bank for the money, they tried to guess the amount involved. Todd figured it to be tens of thousands, but Jim was very decisive when he countered with an explanation the proposed hundreds of thousands.

Adrian had been generous only when it came to dealing with his families living conditions, but nothing else so Beverly didn't really care what the amount was. She only hoped that there was enough to pay off all the debts that Adrian had left behind with her and maybe start a new life for herself, Jennifer, and now Jim. Jim, yes Jim.

She became excited at the thought of being together with him and didn't really notice when the bank official walked up and placed an envelope containing a cashier's check of the total amount of Adrian's account in her hand.

Jim kind of nudged her and she looked up and said, "Oh," and thanked the man as she stood up to go.

Todd said, "Don't you want to see how much it's for?"

Beverly said, "Okay," and. took the checkout of the envelope.

After a long look she sat back down in her chair and in a small voice she said, "Excuse me sir, but I believe there's been some kind of mistake."

The bank executive became exasperated and retorted; "Madam! This bank prides itself and its reputation of never making mistakes. The amount of the account was fifty eight million six hundred and eighty thousand in American dollars exactly! No more and no less.

"We computed our figures as of this morning's Deutschmark standard of exchange so if you feel that you've been cheated somehow. I suggest that you make any complaints you might have to the proper authorities."

He turned with distain and walked away.

Jim spoke up, "Fifty eight million?"

She handed him the check, and after looking at it he passed it to Todd without saying anything. Todd looked at the check, passed it back to Jim without saying anything and Jim passed it back to Beverly.

They continued to sit there in silence until a clerk came and told them that the conference room was needed for another meeting, and if there was no further business would they please leave.

They got up and left the bank, but Jim, having the proper presence of mind, noticed a sign saying Citicorp Intentional Bank and steered them towards the front entrance.

Once inside, he had Beverly open an account and deposit the check. From that point on no matter where she was, all she had to do was find out where the local Citicorp was when she needed money. It was that simple.

That evening they checked out of the hotel and returned to the U.S.A. Beverly went back to New Haven, and Jim and Todd went back to Washington to wait and see if the net they'd cast in Zurich caught anything.

They didn't have to wait long.

One week later Interpol called to report that a man with the proper account number showed up at Zurich-Kroten and tried to withdraw the sum of one million dollars, but had been informed instead of Beverly Perez's' court ordered inheritance.

Since the man did not resemble Adrian Perez, the police were not called in and he left without comment. Jim requested a copy of the bank cameras film from Interpol and they continued to wait.

During this time Jim had put in for a transfer to New Haven so he could be closer to Beverly and Jennifer and about three weeks later he received word that his request had been approved, though he was directed to continue on his assignment with the D.C. police.

That same night he called Beverly to tell her the good news and didn't get an answer at the safe house. So he called the night duty officer in New Haven whom immediately sent a car to check out the house.

Jim waited by the phone believing that was nothing more than a bad phone line.

A couple of hours later the duty officer called back and told him the safe house had been hit.

Jim held his breath as the agent related the body count. All five agents and one unknown assailant were found dead on or around the premises, but there was no sign of Beverly or Jennifer Perez.

Jim, after a few more minutes of conversation with the New Haven agent, pushed down the receiver, called Todd who was in bed, and told him what happened.

They both decided there wasn't much time if they were to track the kidnappers before they got too far away. They rushed to the F.B.I. helipad in D.C. after Jim obtained clearance from his boss who he woke up at home. They were to have a duty officer fly them to New Haven by helicopter.

The flight took about two hours, and when they reach New Haven it was still dark. A car waiting at the airport took them directly to the safe house where Jim and Todd found many people busy at work on the premises.

As they entered the house Jim immediately recognized the female agent, Donna, lying on the floor in front of the door with a pool of blood coming from a hole in her forehead.

She was wearing a nightgown and made Jim wonder just what had gone on there. Todd was saying something to him, and he turned to listen.

"He's come for the money, Jim."

Jim knew that Todd was right, and he told one of the agents in charge to find out who is the biggest executive for Citicorp bank in the area and have him freeze Beverly Perez's bank account before opening time in the morning. A little while later the agent told him that some grumbling Citicorp vice president, rousted out of bed, called this computer database and had someone put a hold on the account. Therefore, no one could have access to the account without first speaking to him personally, and he reminded them that occasionally this is done in cases of suspected fraud.

Jim felt a little easier. As long as Adrian couldn't put his hands on the money he was sure that Beverly and Jennifer would remain alive, but in any event, there wasn't much time left and they had to find them before it was too late.

If it wasn't already too late.

SHORTWAVE: PART THREE

CHAPTER 17

CYCLOPS.

Billy Wayne rode his bike along the block full of abandoned houses and decided to stop for a drink from the water bottle attached to the lower frame of his bicycle. He pulled over to the curb and took a swig.

It was only around 10 am and already he was tired from lugging the large bag of rolled daily papers he usually carried on his shoulder. The sun was unusually warm for this time of day, and he wouldn't be surprised if the temperature had already reached eighty.

"Yep, it sure is gonna' be a warm one," he said as he tilted the bottle and let the cool water pass down his throat.

In front of him stood a fairly large abandoned house built like a temple. It almost reminded him of a church of some kind, but on the facade there was an emblem with a ruler and a compass on it.

Billy thought it might be interesting to explore inside with some friends. He figured he'd stop by Poggy's and Darnell's' and together they'd come back that evening and check out the joint.

He put the bottle away and rode on to the next block where more people resided and resumed his paper delivery job.

Inside the house, S3 watched from the bedroom window as the boy rode away down the street. He wondered if the boy on the bike had seen him through the window and decided to be on the lookout tonight just in case. He'd been waiting for him to leave so he could proceed with his work on the porch outside. This work was essential for their protection, Hans had told him, and he picked up the video camera and wires, opened the front door and went back outside.

He had moved from his old home to this new one over a month ago and never left it during the light of day. He no longer wore the leather jacket because Hans had gotten rid of all the other deadheads and was completely in charge of things with or without it.

It's a funny thing about possession, either you fight it off like a bad cold, or it completely digests you into some eternal abyss from which there is no escape. S3 was completely possessed, and he was afraid.

Hans made him do things that Franz Zimmerman would never have dreamed of, though Hans said it was always in him in the first place. Hans scared him more than anything, and he was always sure he didn't do anything to make angry or upset, because Hans would make his head hurt so bad he would scream for hours.

No, he didn't want to ever make Hans mad again.

He went back inside the house, returning with a step ladder and bracketed the video camera up in the corner of the porch roof.

Running the wires through a hole he had already drilled through the outside wall, he returned inside the house where he hooked up the wire to a TV screen and checked to see that it was working.

The old place still had electricity and that was one of the reasons he had chosen it in the first place even though Hans preferred candles.

The system worked fine and he ran a line down to the basement and hooked up the TV there since that was where he spent most of his time. One day he had single handedly carried a refrigerator down the basement steps and had been surprised at how easy it was.

Hans told him he now had the strength of five men and the power to use it whenever he wanted.

Feeling somewhat perturbed about his looks one day, he asked Hans what he thought about his face and Hans said he liked the way he looked just fine.

So if Hans liked it that was good enough for him, though he did tend to cover it up whenever he went out at night.

He was going to have to dig a hole out back soon and throw what was-left of the body in it except for the head, which Hans wanted kept in the refrigerator.

He approached the man he had hung up by wires, strung from the pipes in the ceiling and removed a knife from his back pocket before cutting a piece of meat from behind the right thigh of the man and returned to the TV monitor. S1 was still alive, but barely.

When S3 cut into him he'd moaned in a state of half consciousness in which he was aware of what was happening to him but unable to do anything about it. S1 slipped deeper into unconsciousness where at least he was far away from the pain and the horror.

He would live through one more night of terror before succumbing to the death he had prayed for ever since the night he had come to the house.

While S3 ate, he turned on the TV monitor and looked at the view outside the house where he could see across the street and beyond. The street was deserted as usual except for the few passing cars that used the street out front as a shortcut to a shopping center a block away.

S3 was short of supplies and figured late that night it would be a good time to visit the store for the things he needed.

Everything seemed quiet out on the street, so he turned off the monitor and went upstairs to the spacious office that acted as his bedroom. He took off his clothes and laid down thinking about the detective he'd been following.

So many times he had come close to getting rid of the man, only to be forestalled time and again, and Hans was beginning to become bothersome and nagging about the issue inside his head.

He tried to close his one eye but could not do it for some time.

He noticed that he didn't seem to sleep much anymore, and even when he did Hans would wake him up, because Hans did not like to sleep.

But this time he did sleep and dreamed he was in hell.

A great demon stood before him with a horrible smile on its face. He had long talons of steel on his fingers, and in one of his hands was a huge iron hammer.

The demon spoke to S3 and demanded, "I thought I told you not to go to sleep?"

The demon raised the hammer and bellowed in a great rage as S3 tried to run, but there was burning fire all around him, and he turned back around just as the demon struck.

S3 jerked to a sitting position in the bed and grabbed his head, wailing in terrible pain.

Billy the paperboy, returned to the Masonic Temple with his two friends, Poggy and Darnell, that same afternoon, and they were in the midst of an argument about who would be the first to go inside.

Darnell being somewhat of a bully and macho man who often disrespected his church going mother, said he would be the first one to go inside, and if they didn't like it he was gonna' punch their lights out. When they got to the back of the house he made Poggy, who was chubby, hold up Billy while he climbed up on Billy to reach the rear window.

Just when he was about to go through the window, he froze. A sudden and terrible scream came from right inside the partially open window.

All three of the boys fell over each other in an effort to get away from the house. Darnell broke his ankle when he hit the ground and became hysterical when his two friends ran away leaving him behind to fend for himself. He called out to them as they disappeared down the street at a speed he didn't think was possible, especially for that fat little Poggy.

Realizing they were not about to come back for him no matter how much he cursed and threatened them, he started to cry like the big baby he really was.

Crawling on his hands and knees, he swore to God that if he could just get away he would never again try to break into a piggy bank, let alone somebody's house!

After having the worst possible time of it, crawling across the street through bushes and stuff while looking over his shoulder most of the way, at last he made it home. The following Sunday he started going to church with his Mamma, much to her great relief.

It wasn't until nightfall before the pain went away and S3 regained his sanity enough to stand up shakily from the bed. He walked to the bathroom in his nakedness where he heaved up the contents of his stomach into the toilet.

Returning to the bedroom, he put on his clothes before leaving the house under the cover of darkness, drove to the shopping center where he broke into the back door of Wal-Mart, and proceeded to load up the trunk of his car with various items. The guard on duty saw the silent alarm going off and made his way to the back door as S3 was returning for more things. The guard pulled his gun and pointed it at S3 who was too far away for the man to get a good look at him.

S3 raised his hands as the guard told him to turn around and put his hands up on the wall next to the door.

S3 did as he was told as the guard approached him and proceeded to search his body for weapons in the dim light. Not finding any he told S3 to turn around.

What he saw before him made him blink, which was the wrong thing to do. S3 struck out swiftly, his fist knocking the gun out of the stunned man's hand and grabbed him in a bear hug and squeezed.

The guard's face was not more than six inches from S3's as he smiled at the man who couldn't tell the difference anyway, because S3s skull was always smiling now.

The guard tried to yell, but his lungs were being crushed, and he could hear the sound of his back breaking in numerous places. He fainted shortly after, and S3 slung him over his shoulder closing the door of the store behind him.

He went to his car and put the luckless man on the backseat before climbing in and driving back to his temple.

When he returned he found a pickup truck parked in front of the building which meant that someone was probably inside. He parked a few doors away and quietly walked up on the porch where he could hear voices inside. He had just installed a new lock and with his key he softly locked the door from the outside and made his way around back and entered the building via the cellar.

Inside the temple two homeboys were piling up some of S3's belongings in the foyer. One of them said to the other, "Yo Hollywood, check this shit out. Somebody's even got a bed in this room over here." The one named Hollywood walked over to where the other man named Skeets was and shined his flashlight into S3's bedroom. They walked in rummaged around and found some jewelry that belonged to S1 and S5 before returning to the foyer.

"I wonder what's in the basement?" Hollywood asked.

"We'll check that out later, man. Let's get this stuff in here to the truck first," Skeets answered.

Each man picked up an arm load of things, and both turned to the door when a voice behind them said, "Good evening gentlemen."

The two men turned around and saw S3, standing not ten feet away from them with his arms down by his side. Skeets angled the flashlight he held in his hand and shined it on S3's face.

"Oh shit ... Skeets whispered. "Open the door."

But Hollywood was paralyzed where he stood looking at S3. "Hollywood, open the damn door!" His homeboy still didn't answer. "Open the freakin' door!"

"It's him. The dude from the Metro. I saw this guy kill some skin heads like they were lice on a rat. Oh God, help us." Hollywood dropped everything in his arms and in jerky movements tried to open the door. S3 continued to stand where he was.

"Uhhh... Skeets?"

"What man?"

"This door won't open."

"What the hell you mean it won't open?" Skeets gurgled, still shining his light on S3's countenance. "Did you try it?"

"Yea, I tried it."

"And what happened?"

"Nothing."

Skeets was confused but had enough courage to say, "All right, now listen here, man. You can have your stuff back, and we'll just leave, no harm done. Alright?"

S3 replied almost in a whisper; "Oh no gentlemen, you must stay! Hans says he must have you for dinner." Skeets was really frightened now.

Hollywood, with a sudden brainstorm, blurted out, "Well man, I ain't really hungry right now, so I'll take a rain check, and maybe one day we'll get together and do a McDonalds or a Burger King or some shit like that. As a matter of fact, my cousin works at Roy Rogers and he can get us free chicken and…"

"Man, will you shut up?" Skeets screamed.

S3 started walking towards the two men.

Skeets threw everything on the floor but the flashlight, which he quickly handed to Hollywood, and dancing around S3 like a boxer, he put his hands up and yelled, "Don't make me hurt you, man."

"Yea Skeets, beat him up like Mike Tyson! I got your back," said Hollywood.

"You got my back? Why the hell don't you do somethin'?" Skeets said as he continued to dance.

"Watch his feet, dog. I saw this dude take out five guys and not break a sweat. Watch his left hook, too."

Suddenly S3 was on him in a blur and struck him unconscious with one rapid left hook to the head.

Hollywood looked at his homeboy lying on the floor and said, "Damn that was quick! I told him to watch for the left hook." He slowly backed up against the door and said, "Look son, I don't know what got into my boy just then with all that golden boy shit... I was just getting' ready to tell him how disrespectful he was actin' and all..."

S3 leaped at him and struck him down, also. He and Hans would eat well for days to come.

CHAPTER 18

The search for Captain Bob Harvey intensified though most of his fellow officers were sure by now he'd gotten himself involved in the Perez affair and could be counted as a casualty of the worst if cliché's cop gone bad, or rogue cop, or what have you. Jim Green was at loss as to what to do next.

He and Todd were still at the house in New Haven, where Beverly and Jennifer had disappeared, when the banks opened the following day, but no one tried to remove the money at any location.

The only thing he could hope for was that the dragnet set up by the local police, the F.B.I., and the Highway Patrol, proved effective in locating the fugitives or Perez. They hoped he would call back with demands of some kind.

A call did come in. However it wasn't from Perez but from the local F.B.I. office. The office informed the agents at the scene that someone had called them claiming to have the woman and the girl and demanded a ransom of over fifty eight million dollars which was to be delivered at an unspecified place and time. They said they would call again with the specifics and hung up.

The fact that they knew about the money and the amount of the ransom could only mean one thing, Adrian Perez was definitely behind the kidnapping.

Jim felt confident they were wasting time waiting for someone to try and remove the money from Citicorp. They would just have to wait for the next call. He also felt sure that Perez would in all likelihood not harm the two females until he got the money. The F.B.I. believed Captain Harvey informed the kidnappers where to find Beverly and her daughter, and Todd knew it was probably best if he and Jim went back to Washington to see what else Harvey may have been up to. There was nothing else they could do there in New Haven, and it was meaningless to remain.

Jim agreed and the two men returned in a couple of hours to police headquarters in D.C. where they were met by the new Captain, Charles Baker.

When Charles Baker arrived at his new assignment he was appalled at the bureaucratic carnage his predecessor had left behind.

Not only was there a backlog of unsolved cases, but more importantly, the moral of everyone at the precinct was critically low. The first thing he did was to establish a daily bull shit session where anyone who wanted to, could air out their feeling about any subject, no matter how trivial.

He believed and rightly so, that the sessions were needed to help everyone come to grips with Captain Harvey's sins and to boost morale. He figured that once things returned to normal the meetings could be done away with.

But to his surprise the daily get together became a healthy and productive mainstay for the precinct and the concept itself was even imitated by some of the other law enforcement agencies.

Captain Baker immediately liked the two men who he'd just met upon their return from New Haven.

After an in depth review of Todd's solid record of service to the department, he believed his predecessor had illegally received credit for much of the work Detective Morrison had done and had deceived the promotion board on at least two occasions about Morrison's inability to meet the testing requirements for promotion to the higher ranks.

He immediately took the case to the Commissioner's manpower committee and one week later Todd was ordered to report to a special session of the promotion board.

For nearly two whole weeks Todd was put through the wringer of written tests, physical exams and verbal inquiry. And when it was all over, he went back to duty feeling unsure about his performance.

After all it wasn't like he'd been given the normal time to prepare for the exam as generally the rule, but still, he was glad to have finally been given a shot at advancement.

For years Bob Harvey had told him there were no slots open in the higher ranks, and he would just have to wait his turn to get his chance. *Oh well, all that was under the bridge now*. At least this new Captain had stood up for him and given him the opportunity that Bob Harvey had denied him for so long.

Jim and Todd continued to work on all the cases pertaining to the Perez investigation notwithstanding the search for the one eyed man who Jim had dubbed as Cyclops, after the name Jennifer had used to describe the man in her dreams.

One month after Jim and Todd had returned to D.C. from New Haven, Captain Baker called them into his office to tell them that the F.B.I. in New Haven had finally gotten another call from the kidnappers and now knew when and where the money would be going.

Captain Baker told them to have their things packed within forty-eight hours as they would be going as a part of the team that would handle the thing. But most of all, the kidnappers had demanded Green specifically be the officer to make the exchange.

Captain Baker looked hard at Jim and said. "We're all a little worried about this one agent Green. You don't have to do this if you don't want to and nobody's gonna' hold you responsible for whatever happens if you don't."

Jim just said, "I wouldn't have it any other way, sir."

"I thought you'd say that. Now there's just one more thing..."

Captain Baker told the two men to follow him and led them outside the precinct down the street to City Hall and into the Commissioner's office where a number of people were waiting, including assorted members of the press.

The Commissioner walked over to Todd and said, "Sergeant Todd Morrison, please come to attention." Todd did as he was told, and the Commissioner continued, "It is my proud duty to officially announce your promotion from the rank of Sergeant to First Lieutenant, with all the duty, privileges, and responsibilities and pay herein, and please accept my apologies for the actions of someone who kept us all fooled for so long.

"I hope that this will at least help to make some amends for all you have done for the people of Washington D.C." He then handed to Todd, amidst applause and flashing cameras, a jewelers box with two silver bars, a florid certificate stating his new rank and promotion, and a First Lieutenants gold badge.

After a moment the Commissioner raised his arms to quiet the applause and announced, "It has also been determined by the promotion board that in six months you will be eligible to test for the rank of Captain.

And I, for one, sincerely look forward to the day that you are running your own precinct in this city because we need more good men like you at the helm."

He shook Todd's hand and everyone applauded again. Todd was somewhat abashed at being the man of the hour and after the hubbub had died down, he left the celebration as soon as was prudent.

Jim and Captain Baker left with him, and on the way back to the precinct, Todd inquired as to why he bypassed the rank of Second Lieutenant. Captain Baker simply stated that Todd's knowledge and experience had been a major factor in their decision to skip him.

When they got back to the precinct, just about the entire place had turned out to congratulate him.

Eventually he tried to return to his desk, but a pretty young female officer took him by the arm and led him to what he recognized as once being the copying room, but had been miraculously transformed into his new office. While he was getting promoted, all his things had been transferred from his old desk to this new office which was also decorated with a banner that said "Congratulations Lieutenant Morrison," and there was a cake with cups and a punch bowl with juice in it on his new desk.

His promotion was just what the precinct needed to regain some of the lost confidence and belief Bob Harvey had left in his wake. And justifiably, a good time was had by all.

Afterwards a number of the revelers, including Jim and Todd, retreated to the local hangout and partied long into the night. The pretty little officer seemed to have taken a shine to Todd remarking as how they were both free and single, while dancing together to the hoots and cat calls of their comrades, they decided to date each other in the near future and before long they exchanged phone numbers.

All in all it had been one hell of a day for Todd Morrison.

Outside, Cyclops waited in the tinted glass car for Todd to leave the bar. Unseen, he had followed the group when they left the precinct and waited outside all evening until the celebration had finally come to an end.

When Todd and Jim left the bar, they said goodnight to everyone and started walking down the sidewalk to Todd's car.

When they got there Todd walked out in the street to the driver's side and was in the process of opening the door when Jim saw a car speeding directly toward him, yelled to lookout. He turned just in time to see the car headed directly for him, and he leapt on the hood of his car as the car slammed the right side of his Mercury where he had just been standing.

The streaking car veered and sloughed off Todd's vehicle, tearing off the bumper in the process, and shot away down the street at a terrific rate of speed.

Todd rolled off the hood and onto the sidewalk where Jim was standing with his weapon drawn, trying to aim at the fleeing car, but the car sped around a corner and disappeared just as he was about to fire. So he put his gun away and helped his friend get to his feet.

Todd stood up and walked back around to the driver's side of the car but couldn't open the door because it was too badly smashed in from the impact.

The two men hailed a cab and went to Todd's apartment where Jim spent the night just in case the driver decided to try and get to Todd at his apartment. The next day Jim went back to his apartment and packed for the upcoming trip while Todd did the same thing before returning to the precinct and assuming his new duties as Deputy Commander.

He met with Captain Baker and informed him of the attempt on his life the previous day and how Jim believed very strongly it was the fugitive they called Cyclops.

The Captain told him, as Deputy Commander, it was his responsibility to make the decisions in the matter before he left town. Todd returned to his new office and called in one of the precincts' better teams and turned this new case over to the two officers with instructions to keep him informed of any development.

The captain would know how to reach him. He also advised them to be careful because the suspect was wanted for a number of killings and was definitely the one who had fired on the two officers at the Rhoads office building.

With that, he took of the rest of the day off to clear up some personal business and then had a late lunch with his new lady friend, Officer Brighty Gordon, before going home for a good night's rest.

The two of them hit it off right from the start and didn't hold anything back from each other. She told him she had always admired him, but never spoke up because of the way Captain Harvey frowned upon that sort of interaction at the precinct.

Todd couldn't believe how easy he found it to be around her and after an enjoyable meal, they left the restaurant, where outside she made him promise that he would take care of himself and call her as soon as he got back from his field assignment. With a small kiss on his cheek, she turned and headed back to work.

Todd stood on the sidewalk and watched her for a while as she walked away, then with a sigh and a smile he turned and went to his newly leased car and with his new lease on life, he headed for home.

It's not an easy thing being tied up with thin wires that cut into your wrists and ankles at the slightest move, once you have learned after God knows how long, you've been unconscious, and that you're lying on the floor in a dark room full of dead people.

But Jamal Walker, better known as Hollywood to most of his friends, at least the ones who called him friend but usually laughed at him behind his back, was trying to make the best of an unbelievably bad situation.

Jamal always figured that one day, one bad day, he would do the wrong thing, at the wrong time, in the wrong place, to the wrong people, for the wrong reason, when he had no right! Yea, he took a chance to make it right on the metro, but the nutcase that killed those skinheads bolted off the train and out of the station before the cops could get there and catch the crazy bastard. Yep no doubt about it, his time was up and his day had finally come.

He tried to sit up, but found that executing the movement to be impossible since his ankles and wrists were tied together behind him, so he just laid there trying to figure out what to do next.

Man! It sure is dark in here. And the smell was enough to make the rats want to pack up and jet.

He tried to peer through the darkness in hopes of seeing his boy Skeets and thought he could vaguely make him out lying to his left about ten feet away.

Jamal whispered, "Skeets... Yo Skeets... can you hear me, man?" When his companion didn't answer, he panicked, thinking Skeets might be dead and yelled out, "Skeeetssss."

"Yo! Will you be quiet! Whacha tryin to do? Bring that bitch down here on us?" Skeets gurgled.

"Oh... Sorry, man."

"Yea, that's right. You are one sorry stank b Hollywood." Skeets spoke angrily while shifting his body around to face the other man.

"I don't know why I let you talk me into this shit! I should have never listened to you and all that crap about this place bein' an easy setup and how we was gonna' make enough from sellin' the crap we found here to stay high for a month. I should have never listened to yo! So keep your mouth shut and let me think!"

Jamal was stung by his friend's words.

It was always like that. He'd go out and find something easy and everyone else would try to take it from him. But let something go wrong and he'd be the one to get blamed for it.

Well, Skeets could go screw himself. He didn't have to lay there and take this shit.

"Hey, Skeets"

"I thought I told you to be quiet."

"Yea? Well blow it out your ass dog! And by the way... your mother's so ugly she makes your father look good! And he's uglier than death."

Skeets choked when he said, "Hollywood, if I get loose I'm gonna' kill you."

Hollywood laughed as he said, "You're gonna kill me? You're gonna' kill me? Yo son! You can't even scratch your ass let alone kill somebody!"

Skeets was silent but Jamal continued. "Do you believe this dude? He's gonna' kill me... Now ain't that somethin' else. You better start worrying about your own ass getting killed... That's what the hell you better do. And what was all that mess you was doin' when you tried to box with that big ugly mf anyway?"

"I tell you, Skeets, you should have seen yourself. Why if you wasn't my boy... I would have dissed you, man. Dude knocked you flat on your ass even after I warned you about his left hook and you gonna' kill me? I don't think so."

"He's gonna' kill somebody..." Jamal muttered at last.

Skeets remained quiet and the two men did not speak other again for quite some time.

A little while later S3 came down the stairs, his clothes rustling in the dark, and lit two candles by the TV monitor.

Hollywood pretended to still be unconscious, but Skeets spoke up and tried to rationalize with S3. "Man... What do you want with us? I know there's some kind of deal or something that I can do to get you to let me go free."

S3 responded by asking; "And what about your friend?"

"Screw him. I'm talking about me. Now what do you say?"

S3 ignored him as he picked up S5's body, carried it upstairs, and out the back door.

Hollywood cruelly laughed in the dark and said, "Ain't that a bitch! Skeets... I thought you and me was boys?"

"You did? Well, now you know," Skeets replied.

"Man that's cold," Jamal said as tears began to swell up in his eyes.

Outside, S3 put S5's body in one of three shallow graves he'd dug the previous night, minus the head. Which he had cut off and placed earlier in the refrigerator. He covered the headless body over with dirt and returned to the basement under the watchful eyes of Hollywood and Skeets, who could plainly watch him in the dimly lit room.

He walked to the back wall and checked to see if S1 was still alive, and finding him dead, he picked up the same hatchet had used earlier on S5. With one stroke, he severed the head from the rest of the torso.

At the sight of the decapitation, Skeets lost all control and openly began to cry, but Hollywood kept his cool. He was a Gulf War vet who had seen worse and kept very still as if he were unconscious.

S3 took the head, which was dripping a large amount of blood, to the frig and put it inside, went back to the torso, removed it also from the basement to the yard out back of the temple, and cast it in another grave before covering it over.

While he was outside Hollywood was trying to get Skeets to pull himself together so that they might think of a way to get themselves out of the mess they were in. But Skeets had wimped out totally and couldn't stop crying. He was no help whatsoever. When S3 returned to the basement, Skeets' crying became a wail as the one eyed creature grabbed him by the back of his shirt and dragged him to the same spot S1 had previously hung and stood him up on his feet before tying the wires to the rope behind Skeets' wrists, pulling him up until his feet were off the floor.

His arms being tied behind him were not able to hold his weight, broke with two loud pops at the shoulders.

Skeets fainted and never felt a thing when S3 cut into him for the first time.

When S3 retreated from the basement for the third time, he left the temple. Hollywood heard the door closed upstairs. Shortly thereafter, a car started up and pulled away into the early morning.

He wriggled his way over to where the machete lay on the floor and grasped the slippery object from behind with his hands.

It was difficult to maneuver the blade so it would cut through the wire but after about an hour, he is able to do just that.

Freeing his hands, he untied his feet and rub his legs vigorously to get the blood circulating in order to stand up.

After a few moments, Jamaal got to his feet and looked around for a minute before walking over to where Skeets hung. He tried to reach up and untied his hands, but found he was too short to do it.

He needed something to stand on. So cautiously, he made his way up the basement steps and back into the foyer where he found a chair. He was about to pick it when from the outside there came a sound of a car pulling into the driveway.

Jamal walked quickly to the rear of the house and found a backdoor, which was unlocked. He opened it up and sucked in the cool, morning air filled with freedom, and began to run as hard as he could towards the inner-city while the first gray hues of the morning's light peeked over the horizon.

CHAPTER 19

It was incredible.

Quite frankly, Jim Green never expected to see the captain and crew of a Harpoon again and was surprised when he learned of the meeting in Miami. The Harpoon would be the vessel to transport them to the point of exchange which happened to be twelve miles off the coast of Cuba and immediately requested his old CWO status to be reinstated. He got his wish.

When he and Todd boarded the ship in Miami, they were met by Captain Dunn and some of the other crew members that Jim had befriended during the last voyage.

Todd had never been on a ship in his life and found the Harpoon to be a source of great wonder to him. Jim introduced him to everyone he knew on board before they got underway. Todd was given the grand tour by the Captain himself who informed him about Jim's exploits on the previous mission.

That afternoon they would make way to Cuba where they would lay off the shore for 24 hours until the exchange of hostages and money, which was really a very good counterfeit that only an expert would be able to discern at first glance, occurred.

Then they would immediately call an assault force lying in wait somewhere nearby, to hopefully surround and capture the kidnappers before they had a chance to get away. At least, that was the plan.

But to their own personal experiences, Jim and Todd both knew that Adrian Perez could be counted on to be somewhat more devious than what the blueprint called for, so they made a contingency plan of their own, just in case.

The prediction would prove fatefully true because unbeknownst to them, Adrian Perez was well aware of the situation.

Adrian Perez sat in a chair overlooking the wide expanse of the Caribbean in the back porch of his luxurious villa in Negril, Jamaica.

He was thinking about events preparing to take place off the shore of Cuba and all the things that had gone wrong to create such a fiasco in the first place.

While he was still in London he made one major change in his plans. He had fallen in love with the stories Etti Samms often told him about her homeland, Jamaica. It was then he decided to make his home there, instead of his prearranged choice, Brasilia.

He went to Sotheby's one month before leaving London and bought the villa he now resided in at an auction for the drastically low price of one and a half million pounds, under his new name and identity, Daniel Thomas, a Brazilian gold dealer.

It had previously blocked when Arab arms dealer who spent more than 10 million and upgrades and no one else at the auction that day was willing to go higher than the stranger with a bandaged face who held the cell booklet containing pictures of the house so tightly in his hands.

The day he left London, he flew to Negril and immediately fell in love with the island's sundrenched beaches and the subtropical lushness of the hills surrounding the island. The topicality reminded him very much of Cuba, and he found it very easy to make himself at home. The day he arrived at the villa, he was met by the staff at Sotheby's had hired for him in his absence a prerequisite for the sale.

The house was magnificent. It was over 20,000 square feet and stood on 150 acres that included, a one and a half mile stretch of private beaches, an oval shaped swimming pool, two tennis courts, a nine hole golf course, stables for 20 horses, and beautifully landscaped gardens all around.

Inside the villa, there were five stately bedrooms and one master suite which contained a Jacuzzi in the bathroom and a solarium with a hot tub directly above the bedroom on the roof, filled with fragrant plants and flowers. The previous owner has spared no expense to create for himself, and indirectly for Adrian, a veritable paradise in paradise.

Quickly he became known around the island as a playboy and usually had his pick of local and foreign women.

In Nagril, there was a Club Med that he frequently visited, filled with Americans and Europeans who he invited to parties he hosted at the villa every Friday at midnight by the oval pool, replete with caterers and local reggae bands.

These parties made him particularly esteemed by the local government due to the number of people employed and the police patrolling the road around his estate, in jeeps, were generally more than enough to give him ample security.

In just a few short months, he had created for himself a life of great luxury and romance he only once dreamt about. But as someone once said, there was trouble in paradise.

A little more than a month ago, he went to Zürich in order to replenish his depleted accounts and learned that Beverly had somehow laid claim to the fortune he thought he had sufficiently secreted away.

No one could ever imagine his surprise that day and immediately called S5 to find out what the hell had happened. S5 apprised him of the entire affair and also told him where to find the woman and the girl.

He couldn't believe how these people had managed to meddle in his affairs. But they would not get away with it.

Some time ago, he had imported S2 and S4 from the U.S.A. As his personal bodyguards, they quickly devised a plan to kidnap the two females in order to get the money back. The three of them proceeded to an address in New Haven, Connecticut, were S5 had told them the two women would be.

Being forewarned about the number of agents on guard, they were well armed with hand weapons with silencers attached and semi-automatic rifles.

Dressed in dark clothing and ski masks, they attacked the house stealthily in the late evening and easily took out the two agents in the unmarked car parked out front before proceeding to split up to best infiltrate the residence from different places.

Adrian went into the front of the house while S2 and S4 entered from the rear. Agent Donna Landers was doing her nightly rounds and was about to check the bedroom that contain the two women when she heard a noise at the front door.

Knowing that no one else was supposed to be moving around, she retreated to her own bedroom and picked up her Smith & Wesson 9 mm from the night table and proceeded down the stairs.

She saw someone gently pushed the door open and waited until the masked person entered before saying, "Put your weapons down on the floor and put your hands on top of your head."

Adrian was surprised at being caught so easily and did as he was told. When Donna got to the bottom of the stairs she was just about to reach for the intercom located by the front door when she heard a soft snap and a bullet tore through her back and right through her heart.

She spun around and fired in the general direction of the sound before falling to the floor, where she quickly lost consciousness. S2 the S4 entered to the rear of the house and found two male guards asleep on bunks in the breakfast room and shot them in the head at point-blank range.

S4 silently walked into the dining room and out into the hallway where he saw a female holding a gun and Adrian by the front door, and he shot her in the back. But amazingly the woman spun around and fired back at him. The bullets caught S2 in the forehead, and he too crumbled dead to the floor. Adrian picked up his weapon and fired point blank into Donna's forehead to ensure she was dead.

Adrian and S4 continued their sweep of the house and found the two females who they'd bound and gagged.

S4 went to retrieve the stolen van, and they had parked around the corner and drove it to the rear of the house where one by one they deposited the two females inside. As they left the house, the phone rang, letting them know that there was little time to waste.

They drove to Mystic Seaport were Adrian's 50 foot cigarette speedboat was secretly moored, and putting the females in the cabin, S4 turned on the engines and swiftly headed out to the open sea.

The boat could do better than 70 miles an hour on the water and made it back to Jamaica in less than 48 hours.

During the journey, Adrian never said a word to Beverly or Jennifer, and it was S4 who made the phone call to the FBI office in New Haven from a portable handheld telephone, when Adrian took the controls and bought the boat in close to the mainland for that purpose.

Adrian felt other than losing S2, it had been a successful undertaking and was now prepared to launch stage two of his plan to recover his fortune. Well aware of the authority's plan to try and trap him during the exchange, he devised what he considered an almost perfect response.

But there was one thing S5 didn't tell them about, which was a last-minute decision to use counterfeit instead of real money, because he would meet his death before he could find out about it in time to inform Adrian.

As Adrian sat overlooking the Caribbean, he considered the consequences of failure this time as being remote. He had no intentions of leaving behind any more loose ends and believed that his plan had taken into consideration all possible contingencies. It was foolproof.

The authorities would bring the money to a prearranged location just outside the twelve mile limit of Cuba's coastline, where Beverly and Jennifer would be waiting in a dinghy on the water, tied with explosives. The money was to be packed in boxes and contained in a nylon net on a small floating barge where one man would also wait to pick up the two females and no vessels could be within five miles of the barge or the dinghy, or else boom, and the woman and girl were dead.

At the appointed time, a helicopter would fly over the barge and pick up the money with a hook and fly towards Cuba were Adrian had used his contacts to make a deal for the use of a particular airstrip secretly located somewhere in the mountains.

When the helicopter had disappeared from sight, then and only then would the agents be able to pick up Beverly and Jennifer from the dinghy. At least that was the plan as far as authorities were concerned. He had already made sure F.B.I. agent Jim Green was the man on the barge and in reality had no intentions of allowing him or the two females to survive one more time.

As soon as the helicopter picked up the money, a sniper would take out Jim Green and the dinghy would be exploded, leaving authorities with nothing but three more dead bodies.

They could chase the airship into Cuba if they dared, but would cost them and lives because everyone knew Castro's hatred towards the West knew no bounds and he would most certainly logic on her attack or even openly declare war against the U.S. for the intrusion.

They would indeed be hard-pressed to move against him while he was in Cuba, and he would have plenty of time to transport his money back to Jamaica before returning there himself.

Yes, the plan was foolproof. He rose from his chair to go prepare for the action.

The Harpoon made its way lazily through the deep blue waters of the Caribbean to the rendezvous point off the coast of Cuba with a small cable barge in tow.

Jim and Todd made use of their free time during the voyage packing all the counterfeit money into collapsible boxes the Coast Guard had provided for them. Once again Jim was back in the uniform of a chief Warrant officer second class, and he enjoyed the friendly kidding that Todd frequently bombarded them with.

This time, if such a thing were possible, the food in the galley was even better. The chief cooks mate seemed to outdo himself. For lunch the first day the men on board were treated to Alaskan king crab legs and shrimp smothered in water, served with scallop potatoes and fresh corn on the cob. That night for dinner, prime rib was the main course with baked potatoes and broccoli in a cheese sauce, with chocolate mousse as a dessert.

At dinner, Todd verbally demanded how in the hell the Coast Guard could eat so well when as a Navy sailor he had never enjoyed such meals. The sailors explained that on many occasions they intercepted smuggled goods on the high seas and always got the first crack at whatever the manifest was. Whether it was clothing, weapons, or food, the Coast Guard was first in line to lay claim and often distributed some of the goods to victims of hurricanes and floods.

It was one of the not so publicized benefits of being a member of the Coast Guard and the service preferred to keep it that way.

As Todd was being served by the cook, he inquired as to how fresh the bread was and immediately regretted it. The cook stopped what he was doing and proceeded to give Todd such a cussing out that he can only stand there with his mouth wide open until Jim led him away to a seat at one of the tables to howls from the members of the crew, this time joined in by Jim.

He soon explained to Todd that it was only the Chief's way of welcoming new people on board ship and the same thing had happened to him, but Todd didn't seem to be impressed and was dog-faced the rest of the evening.

The Harpoon reached its destination the following day and Jim was deposited on the barge in a wet suit, and after being cast loose, the Harpoon turned north and disappeared over the horizon.

Jim stood next to the boxes of counterfeit money under the hot afternoon sun and waited.

After about twenty minutes a boat driven by two men appeared at a distance towing a dinghy with Beverly and Jennifer inside and pulled up within fifty meters of the counterfeit laden barge before casting the dinghy loose and quickly heading west.

Jim could see that the Beverly and Jennifer were all right but were encumbered by their hands and feet being tied behind them.

But there was nothing he could do about that and as soon as the boat disappeared over the horizon, Jim dove into the water. Beverly and Jennifer were likewise grabbed by two men wearing scuba gear who surfaced next to the dinghy a few seconds later and pulled them screaming into the water just as Adrian's helicopter appeared, headed rapidly in their direction from the west.

Adrian could see what was happening through his field glasses from his position in the helicopter and reached for the remote control device in the bag next to him and depressed the button detonating the charges surrounding the small craft and exploding the dinghy in a thousand pieces into the air.

Afterward, there was no sign of life on the water anywhere, and the helicopter lowered down to the barge where S4 jumped out and attached a cable from the airship to the net holding the boxes of counterfeit money. He jumped back on the helicopter just as a missile from one of the Harpoons long range guns exploded next to the barge sending water in plumes into the air, drenching the airship and S4 before the helicopter turned to flee west into Cuban air space in the face of the approaching Coast Guard vessel.

They would make good their escape. For the time being.

Sixty meters below the surface, Jim, Beverly, and Jennifer were breathing oxygen through air tanks and waited along with three frog men until the Harpoon was directly overhead before surfacing and being helped aboard ship.

Everyone was unharmed except for momentary loss of hearing caused by shock waves from the explosion, which they had just been able to escape. The Harpoon would not follow the helicopter to Cuba and turned north east towards the mainland of the United States.

After being checked out and released from the ship's sickbay, Beverly and Jennifer recounted their month-long captivity to Jim, Todd and Captain Dunn in the galley over lunch.

Beverly was frightened. She had been bound and gagged on a fast moving boat for hours since the men had come for her and Jennifer at the safe house in New Haven, N.Y. The house turned out to not be so safe after all. She was sure that Adrian was behind their abduction but had yet to see him, though she felt in her heart he was somewhere on the boat.

After what seemed like days, the boat came to a stop and they were taken aboard a much larger vessel where they were cast into a small engine room and spent the next weeks in the semi-darkness except for an occasional guarded walk at night up on deck.

They were fed three times a day, and there was a small bathroom just down the passageway they could use.

One day after demanding to talk to whoever was in charge, Beverly was able to talk to Adrian from behind the closed door of her dank and dark prison but could not see him.

Like a voice in the night she heard him say, "And how is my beautiful American family today?" He laughed and continued, "Did you miss me, my dear wife and child?"

Beverly answered, "Why have you done this to us? What did I ever do to you to deserve what you have done to me and my children?"

Adrian suddenly became angry and exploded, "What have you done? What have you done? I'll tell you what you've done *mujer*, you meddled in affairs that did not concern you and took what was not yours to take. The money is mine! Do you understand, bitch? It's mine," he shouted at her through the door.

Jennifer started to cry and Beverly asked him to go away which he did, but not before saying, "Let me explain something to the both of you. This time you will both die, and I will be the source of your death."

And in a sweet voice he purred, "I have also made sure that your precious F.B.I. man, Jim Green, will die right along with the both of you."

Jennifer gasped and shouted, "Nooo! "

Beverly cried. "Please Adrian... I beg you! Don't do this to Jennifer! She's your own flesh and blood!"

Adrian laughed cruelly and replied, "Don't expect mercy due to a mere accident of birth. You might say it's just her bad luck to have me as her father."

Adrian turned and left and that was the last time they had any more contact with him.

There was never a guard around when the hatch was closed and locked, so they could pretty much find things to do together to make the time go by and Jennifer proved to be good at making up games to keep them occupied.

She always seemed to keep pretty good spirits because she believed that Jim would come for them and this time Beverly did not doubt for a minute that she was correct in her assumption.

Jennifer and Jim seem to have a psychic awareness of one another that was strictly the domain of the two of them, and Beverly didn't feel any rivalry in the least. In fact she took heart in Jennifer's clairvoyant connection with Jim which made their imprisonment much more bearable.

In the past year Jennifer had matured well beyond her age and proved to be quite capable of adapting to their plight and Beverly increasingly found herself admiring this little girl who had been through so much yet still was full of spunk and determination.

Adrian was certainly wrong about her, she knew, for Jennifer was unequivocally no accident of birth and somehow she knew the man would live long enough to regret those words.

All in all, their existence wasn't too bad, and they both had each other to count on, which was the most important thing.

The only real problem was the lack of bathing facilities, which they overcame by periodically washing their bodies and clothes from the sink in the bathroom when they were allowed.

Then one day they were transported by truck, to a small shack on a beach somewhere and kept there until the morning when they were tied hand and foot and put into the dinghy. There the story ended.

Captain Dunn said he figured that the two females had been kept on one of those deserted transport ships that dot the Cuban Coast line and had been very lucky not to have been killed during the explosion.

It had been Jim and Todd's contingency plan that saved the day. If Jim had not dived in the water, the divers were instructed not to attempt to free the women.

And Captain Dunn along with everyone else knew that Adrian was ready to kill all three of them once he had got the money.

But now the ring around the man had definitely grown tighter and Jim had a feeling that the time was drawing near when there would be nowhere left in the world for Adrian Perez to hide. And when that time came he would be there waiting. And this time-there would be no escape.

CHAPTER 20

Jamal Walker sat in the living room of the house belonging to the parents of his girlfriend, Iris Woods, and cried. Iris was the mother of his two kids and at the moment she was in the kitchen arguing with her father about his being there. Her father hated Jamal with a passion, and he could hear their shouting filter down the hallway into the living room.

Her father said, "How many times I got to tell you I don't want that nigga' in my house no mo'? He ain't nothin' but a crack head and he's gonna' drag you down with him if he can!"

"But Pops!" he heard Iris reply. "I tell you... there's... there's something wrong... really wrong this time! I can't explain it... he just ain't his old self!"

"Well that's bound to be a great improvement, but he still ain't staying here I don't care if the goddamn boogey mans after him, that's his tough luck!" Her father replied with vehemence. "Now either you go back in there and tell that good for nothin' nigga' to get the hell out of my house, or I will damn it."

Jamal wiped his eyes and stood up, walked to the front door, opened it and stepped outside, gently closing the door behind him as Iris continued to fight with her father on his behalf. She was a good sweet woman and he dogged her for a long time but that shit was all over with.

Here was the one person, the only one, who even gave him a bit of respect, and he knew he didn't deserve her, but now he thanked his lucky stars that through it all she still loved him and stuck by him.

It was a week since he'd left Skeets behind in the old house up near the Creek Tree shopping mall, and now he knew exactly who he was dealing with. He'd learned on the news that the one eyed man's name was Franz Zimmerman, and there was a one hundred thousand dollar reward for information leading to his capture. Jamal knew exactly where he was.

He now had a chance, a chance of a lifetime, a chance to show Iris, their children, and her parents that he was more than just a broken down Gulf war vet and a drug user. A chance to make good. He wondered how many lives he might save with one phone call to the authorities, if that call resulted in the capture of the creature known as Franz Zimmerman. But that was a big if.

Then he thought, maybe he could show them what he was really made of if he could get the drop on that monster Franz Zimmerman. But wait! He would need a gun. Iris's father had a gun, but that was out of the question now, so he had to figure out some other way to pull it off.

As he walked down the street, he remembered that one of the crack heads he knew named Spoon was always braggin' about his semi-automatic, though Jamal had never actually seen it. As he thought about this, going to Spoon's house, it was going to be problem because it wasn't like he still wasn't an addict. He was, and he knew it.

Every day it was a struggle to stay away from the people and the places where the dope could be found, and it had been very difficult to remain drug free. But these last few days, he had done exactly that, and it gave him a feeling of real accomplishment.

It had been a year since he had gone so long without even a joint or something, and Jamal wondered if something had changed inside of him.

He dug his hands into his pockets and held his head a little higher as he walked towards Spoon's neighborhood as evening began to darken the skies to the east.

Spoon was home when he got there and opened the door to let him in. As Jamal walked in, the sickeningly sweet pungent smell of crack assaulted his entire being.

Spoon said, "Heeeyyy, Hollyyywood! What up son! I got somethin' special that's happinin'."

Spoon walked over to a wooden table in his apartment, picked up a small vial, turning it upside down in his hand, and placed crystaline rock of crack cocaine on to the top of a burned crack pipe. He turned to Jamal and said, "This one's on me, brother."

Right then and there, Jamal had a fight with the devil. He was sure he was going to lose when he heard a voice outside of him say; "Sure, man, sure... but right now I need to borrow your piece to get some money from a dude that owes me, and then I'll be back."

Spoon looked at Jamal kind of funny and asked, "Uhh... just how much does this dude owe you?"

Jamal thought for a second then shrugging his shoulders said, "A hundred thousand dollars."

Spoon backed away from Jamal, turned, and lifted up a sofa cushion revealing an Uzi automatic with an extra cartridge underneath. He picked up both items and handed them to Jamal and said, "Go get paid, my brother."

Jamal stuck the weapon in his waistband and put the cartridge in the pocket of his field jacket, turned, and left the apartment.

When he got outside, it was already dark, and he stopped by a phone booth to made one call before continuing.

He walked silently in the direction of Creek Tree, where the old house stood, with a purpose on his face as dark as the night.

The evening air was filled with the sounds of nocturnal creatures that waited until the moon was overhead to seek out and feed upon the weak and the frightened.

S3 was one of those creatures of the night.

S3 drove his car around in the immediate vicinity of the house where Detective Todd Morrison lived hoping to catch the man unaware. But once again Morrison didn't show up.

S3 headed his car back in the direction of the temple, afraid of what Hans might do, or make him do, because of his latest failure and was barely able to contain his fear.

He pulled into the driveway of the temple and parked. As he got out of the car and walked towards the house, Jamal Walker made his move.

He'd been hiding along the side of the house,
which he tried to enter without much success, and
when S3 got out the car he stepped out from the
shadows with the Uzi pointed at the thing that now
only vaguely resembled a man.

Jamal spoke, "Yo! What up?"

S3 stopped in his tracks and looked in the direction
of Jamal and said in his throaty German accent, "Mr.
Hollywood, isn't it? I was wondering when you would
return. Your friend missed you dearly, and you could
say he was consumed by your absence."

S3 slowly began to close the distance between him
and the thin black man. Jamal yelled; "What the hell
you think you doin'?"

S3 stopped and stood waiting for Jamal's next
move.

Jamal said, "Now lay your ugly ass down on the
ground before I get nervous and this gat goes off in
what's left of your face. Trust me."

S3 did as he was told just as the night was suddenly
lit up with the flashing lights and wailing sirens of the
many police cars that approached the house from all
directions.

Jamal smiled and said to S3, "Got you, Franz..."

"It seems that you do, Mr. Hollywood... at least for
now.'" S3 acknowledged, as he lay patently on the
ground.

Police cars raced up the driveway and on the grass
as Jamal put the Uzi on the ground and raised his arms
in the air. The officers got out their cars with shotguns
pointed at him and S3.

S3 was handcuffed and put into a police van and as
the doors were closed and locked, he unexpectedly
wailed from inside the vehicle before it pulled away;

followed by at least five police cars. The wail was a horrible sound that sent chills up the backs of everyone.

Jamal remained at the scene and was questioned before leading the police on a tour of the house and its dark secrets. He was very candid with the investigators that arrived shortly thereafter and admitted breaking into what he thought was an abandoned house.

He had to tell his story all over again to two more officers who had arrived much later.

When Todd and Jim checked in with the precinct from the airport, after their return from their assignment aboard the Harpoon, they were shocked to find out that Franz Zimmerman had been captured.

They were given directions to the temple and rushed to the scene where they were told a bizarre story by a thirty-five year old drug abuser. Then they learned about the grotesque discoveries the arriving officers made inside the house, in the basement, and in the backyard. It was almost too much.

They had to get Jamal Walker's story on tape, and once the crime lab got there, they returned to the precinct with Jamal, as the news vans began to arrive on the scene. Word had spread about the capture, and at the precinct they were met by a huge throng of reporters who wanted to question Jamal about how he was able to single handedly capture one of the most feared and dangerous men in recent memory.

Jamal stood for a moment in front of all the lights and the reporters with their microphones, cameramen, and live satellite feeds and explained, "I did it to save my life and for my girl, Iris, and our two kids." He paused for a moment to look out over the now very quiet crowd of reporters. "When you're a hardcore drug addict like I am, there ain't nothin' you won't do to get high over and over again. And... and... this dude... this monster, was gonna' eat me just like crack does. And then I knew what crack really was all about. So I figured that if I could go back there to that house of death and deal with him and live to tell about it, then I could face my addiction and live to tell about that, too. And now more than ever I just want to live and try to be a good man to Iris and the kids."

He turned and walked into the precinct flanked by Todd and Jim as the throng of reporters erupted into applause.

It wasn't until the next morning that a very tired Jamal Walker, formerly known as Hollywood, was deposited in front of the home of Iris Woods with an envelope containing a cashier's check for one hundred thousand dollars held tightly in his left hand. Iris was standing at the front window and watched him as he walked up the steps, where her father was waiting at the door, and began to cry as the two men shook hands for the very first time.

CHAPTER 21

The capture of Franz Zimmerman was sensational news copy all over the world. His was one extraordinary story, to say the least, and even though the TV shows couldn't get him, they could get this Jamal Walker if the price was right and only with the approval off his new manager, who was also his new father in-law.

There was even talk about a made-for-TV movie about Jamal's life. But the story was far from over.

Todd and Jim went to see S3 in his special room at the prison hospital where he was being held a couple of weeks after his capture.

He had refused all offers to reconstruct the flesh on his face and was almost constantly restrained by leather straps in his bed and guarded twenty four hours by correctional officers armed with loaded shotguns.

He was frightening to behold and the other prisoners in the hospital passed around a petition demanding that he be sent somewhere else. Amazingly he had already confessed all his crimes to the authorities, and it was only a matter of clearing up a few loose ends that brought Todd and Jim to the prison to see him.

As Todd entered the room, S3 spoke; "Ahh... Detective Morrison, how nice to see you."

"I can't say the feeling's mutual, Zimmerman," Todd replied as he and Jim took seats in the room.

"You know Detective Morrison, you have caused us quite a lot of trouble and killing you was still unfinished business at the time of my recent apprehension. I will have to get around to you sooner or later."

Jim was shocked at what the man was saying. *This Franz Zimmerman has to be totally unwound to say such a thing.*

But Todd only smiled and said, "Listen Franz, how long did you work for Adrian Perez, and can you tell us where he is right now?"

But S3 replied by saying; "By the way, Detective Morrison, how is that plump little *Freulein* you've been seeing lately? Is she as sweet as she looks to be?

Todd stood up and said, "Come on, Jim, there's nothing more we can do here."

The two men rose to go, and S3 started to laugh as they walked to the gate and were let outside the room.

Two weeks later, Todd and Jim got a message from Interpol that the counterfeit money was beginning to turn up in Jamaica and the Jamaican authorities had pinpointed a couple of suspects though no arrests had been made as of yet.

The two officers found themselves preparing for yet another plane ride, and they took along with them copies of the photos they'd received from the Zurich-Kroten bank of the man who tried to withdraw money from the Adrian Perez account in hopes that this could be the man they were looking for. They also took with them copies of Perez's fingerprints.

In Kingston, they were met by the police chief who took them to headquarters.

An Interpol agent was waiting for them with recent photos of the two suspects in question and they matched perfectly with the pictures of one of the suspects whose name was Daniel Tomas. The other suspect, a Mr. Drexler, worked for Daniel Tomas at his estate.

The Jamaican authorities wanted to catch their two suspects red-handed and told Todd and Jim that following evening Mr. Tomas would be throwing one of his famous parties at the estate in Negril, and he always made a currency exchange prior to paying for the services involved in the party.

The next day Jim and Todd, along with Jamaican police, were hidden behind a back door to the bank, where S4, or Mr. Drexler as he was known, came to exchange American currency for Jamaican. Daniel Tomas was not with him.

So they decided to let Drexler make the transaction and decided to make their arrests later on that evening during the party.

Daniel Tomas was known in Negril as the consummate host. He was always making sure that his guest's needs were well taken care of. Whether it was the right kind of food, a drink that needed to be refilled, or maybe the right room in the main house to find the right drug, you might say he was Johnny on the spot.

It was a warm evening in Negril, and the trade winds that seemed to blow continuously during the day had died down to just a few small breezes. The moonlit sky was filled with stars, and the picture was completed by the appearance of an occasional cloud.

As Adrian made his rounds among the guests by the pool that night, he noticed the police Chief from Kingston was among the revelers. He approached the man thinking that maybe he was looking for a payoff of some kind and shaking the officer's hand, he said, "It is good to see our esteemed Chief of police in attendance enjoying himself. Is there something I might be able to do for you? Maybe something I can get you?" It was then that Adrian noticed there were two other men with him. He felt sure he'd seen one of them before but couldn't quite place the face.

As he studied the man trying to make the connection, Todd smiled back at him and said; "Hello Adrian, this is some party you're having, but I'm afraid the party is over now."

Suddenly there were sounds of complaints from the guests as a multitude of policemen invaded the premises and roughly shuttled people out to the road. The police Chief took out a pair of handcuffs and savagely pulled Adrian's arms behind him and snapped on the cuffs.

Adrian began to struggle and the Chief knocked him in the head with his fist bringing a yelp of pain from his prisoner.

Todd said to Adrian, "I guess they're not as friendly here as we are back in, D.C."

Then the realization hit Adrian. "You!" he shouted.

"Yes, me," Todd said. "You look a lot different now Adrian, but you still have the same bad manners as before. The name is Detective Morrison, remember? Oh, by the way, let me introduce you to Agent Jim Green of the F.B.I." At that moment there was sporadic gunfire from inside the house and shortly thereafter, a policeman came out of the house and told them that the man named Drexler had been killed trying to pull a gun on some of the officers. Pest control had been all but obliterated.

Adrian Perez was extradited back to the U.S. where he stood trial in Washington, D.C. for over three hundred counts of murder and espionage. Coincidentally, Franz Zimmerman's trial was held at the same time, though the two men never saw each other during their trials.

Jim was released from his assignment with the D.C. police and reassigned with the New Haven Bureau where Beverly and Jennifer were living permanently.

During his trial, Adrian was held at the Maryland County Detention center where one day a prisoner was transferred from Allenwood Federal prison, for a court date concerning the reduction of his sentence. He was made aware of Adrian's presence and vowed revenge.

One night as Adrian was eating dinner with the rest of the prisoners in the mess hall. Ruiz Alvarez walked up behind Adrian as he ate and hissed in his ear; "This is for my sister, *chinga!*"

He plunged a sharpened screwdriver into Adrian's upper back, yanked it out and shoved it in again before disappearing into a crowd of prisoners leaving the mess hall.

Adrian arched his back and tried to scream. The men around him distanced themselves from the wounded prisoner, and a guard noticed that he was gagging on what she thought was his food.

As she approached him she saw the screwdriver protruding from his back and blew her whistle.

Adrian, having passed out, was taken to the prison hospital where the screwdriver was removed, but fearing severe internal injuries, it was decided that he should go immediately to one of the trauma units' downtown in D.C. along with another patient who was complaining that he could not see out of his one good eye.

As the three officers and a doctor who would be going along for the ride prepared the patients for transport, a nurse read their names out loud over the intercom to the guard on duty at the outside gate.

S3 stiffened in his bed when he heard the name of Adrian Perez being called out by the nurse, but remained silent as two of the officers shackled him and led him out to the hospital vehicle, putting him on a seat in the back next to the stretcher carrying Adrian Perez, who was unconscious.

He smiled when one officer and the doctor got in with him and Adrian, while the other two officers sat up front. The ambulance pulled out of the prison yard with the lights flashing.

The trauma team was waiting for them at Cedar Sinai, but after two hours one of the doctors called the prison to report that the ambulance never showed up.

After a futile search for the missing vehicle, a massive manhunt was initiated but proved fruitless.

Once again the two mass murders were on the loose and there would be hell to pay and the devil, too.

Shortwave: Part Four

THE ANGEL AND THE DEVIL TOO!

CHAPTER 22

A lot of heads rolled following that fateful night when Adrian Perez and Franz Zimmerman made their escape from the prison system.

There were a number of inquiries as to why the two men were in the same facility to begin with and why they were being transported together to a downtown hospital with only three guards and no backup.

The prison warden stated there was no reason why the two men should not have been in his prison because they were both on trial and the Detention Center was primarily a holding cell for prisoners awaiting trial.

He also said that it was common procedure to transport hospital cases in the manner that had been chosen.

Nonetheless, he was the first one asked to resign his position to appease a worried and scared populace.

Then the prisons Deputy Administrator who wrote the order to transport the two men and the Captain who implemented the order were both relieved of their duties along with a few more unlucky souls.

The ambulance was found ditched in a small ravine outside of Philadelphia, a few days later without any of its passengers, though investigators did find the arm and leg shackles that were used to bind Franz Zimmerman in the back of the vehicle.

There were telltale signs of a scuffle and the floor was covered in blood. There really wasn't enough to piece together a scenario of what had happened and the police Commissioner was asked by the mayor of D.C., who was also feeling victimized by the whole affair, to put his best people on the case.

So once again the F.B.I. was asked to re-assign Agent Jim Green to Police Central Precinct in Washington, to work alongside Lieutenant Todd Morrison in the hopes that the two men could once again deliver the goods and bring the fugitives back into custody.

Jim was on vacation and enjoying the company of the newly divorced Beverly Stokes (she had taken back her maiden name) and her daughter Jennifer.

They had flown back down to Jamaica together to take stock of the villa which had been turned over to her and were enjoying a much needed rest when they received a call from the local police.

Beverly had taken the call in the main house and rushed out to the small cottage by the pool where Jim was staying and told him about the escape. The

Jamaican government immediately sent a detachment of reserves to protect the house and its occupants.

But Jennifer told the arriving solders that they didn't have to stay, because the Cyclops would not be coming after them. The Commandant of the small force smiled at the strange little girl and went about positioning his men around the grounds of the estate.

But Jim and Beverly did take her serious, very serious.

Jim asked her what it was she knew and she said, "I meant to tell you the other day about the dream I had, but since I didn't think it really involved us I guess I just forgot."

Beverly smiled at her daughter; knowing she didn't want to see Jim leave them again, ever.

Jennifer told them; "In the dream the Cyclops is in a big forest and it's cold. He's got that man that used to be my father with him, and they are waiting." At that point she stopped and looked at Jim and said, "I know you have to go. I guess it is your duty, but this time Cyclops knows who to expect and it's you he's waiting for. You and that other man, Mr. Morrison, and if you go this time, I can't tell if you'll come back." She turned and walked away, headed toward the stables.

Jim talked for a while with Beverly and then made his call to the U.S. He was ordered back to Washington, D.C. to take up the chase once again along with Todd Morrison, just like Jennifer predicted.

As he was packing his few belongings, Jennifer came running into the cottage almost out of breath and blurted out, "Can I go too, Jim? I can help you find them, I know I can."

"Yes, you probably could Jen-Jen... but I don't think the bureau would take too kindly to endangering the life of such a sweet little girl, and I love you too much to let that happen."

He walked over to her and put his arms around the youngster who looked up and said, "I'll be with you in my dreams."

Todd Morrison lay in bed beside Brighty Morgan, and he could feel the warmth of her body making him excited all over again. They had gone out together on a dinner date the previous evening and with one thing leading to another; they wound up at her little house in Bethesda in the wee hours of the morning,

She lived with her mother and her two children by a previous marriage, who he thought were all asleep until there was a small knock on the bedroom door and a little five-year-old girl in a yellow bathrobe and slippers opened the door and walked into the room holding a huge pink stuffed elephant close to her body:

She walked over to his side of the bed and stopped and stared at him. "Who are you?" she asked looking scared as tears filler her eyes.

Brighty looked into her daughter's eyes reassuringly. "This is Todd, honey. Mommy is okay, and he is a good friend of mine. Sorry to scare you with him being here. I asked him to stay to meet you, Eric, and Grandma.

Todd looked at her and replied, "I'm Todd. What's your and your elephant's name?"

"Oh..! Well, I'm Jean and this is my best friend Alfred, and he likes to play games and everything, but Granny doesn't like it when he sits on the breakfast table so I put him in the seat next to me when we eat breakfast. Do you have a pink elephant, too?"'

Todd answered, "No, but I have a giraffe."

"Well what's his name?"

Todd felt Brighty move behind him and wrap her arms around his waist, under the covers. She questioned him, "Well, what is his name Todd? Inquiring minds want to know!"

The little girl smiled and said, "Good morning, Mommy."

"Good morning, Jean."

"Mommy?"

"What is it, hon?

"Granny wants to know if you guys are coming to breakfast."

"Tell her we'll be right there."

Jean asked, "Will you bring the giraffe over to visit Alfred sometime?"

"Yes, I'll bring him over very soon."

Jean smiled again and walked to the door softly closing it behind her as she left the room.

Todd turned around in the bed to face Brighty. He said, "I guess your mother knows I'm here, huh?"

Brighty giggled and said, "It's all your fault!"

"What do you mean it's all my fault?"

She answered, suddenly becoming serious, "Well, if you hadn't made me fall in love with you, you wouldn't be here, would you?"

Todd moved closer to Brighty and said, "I wonder what's for breakfast?"

Brighty kissed him. "How's that for starters?"

It was sometime before the two lovers made it down to the kitchen where breakfast was already in progress. When they walked in together, hand in hand, Jean and her brother Eric began to giggle uncontrollably.

Brighty's mother stood up and offered her hand to Todd before speaking, "Well, I finally get to meet the famous Mr. Morrison..."

That seemed to set the kids to giggling even louder.

"It seems that you're all I've been hearing about from my daughter for the longest time. Won't you please sit down and join us?"

Todd whispered to Brighty, "What does she mean for the longest time?" as he pulled out one of the chairs at the table.

When he sat down he felt a large object underneath him and jumped up in surprise. He turned and saw Jean's elephant Alfred staring up at him accusingly. Everybody broke out in a wild laughter that made Todd feel right at home. He sat down and began to get to know this wonderful group of people who seemed to like him so thoroughly.

The sun shone through the kitchen window and seemed to light up Brighty's face, which he couldn't keep his eyes off, their lovemaking still fresh as if in a dream. He thought someone was saying something to him and he turned to see who was speaking, but the group just started to laugh again and Brighty seemed to blush.

Later on Todd was helping the kids and their grandmother clear the dishes off the breakfast table while Brighty checked in with the precinct from a phone in the living room.

When she came back into the kitchen her face was drawn and had lost its color. His eyes questioned her and she reluctantly said, "You'd better call in Todd, something's happened." She turned and walked away from him.

He used the phone on the kitchen wall and listened as the Captain told him all about the escape and how he and Jim Green had been ordered by the Commissioner to head up the search for the escapees.

When Todd hung up the phone he figured that life was playing some kind of cruel trick on him had seriously considered resigning from the force. He sat down with Brighty and discussed doing just that.

Brighty had told them he could never really be happy if he wasn't doing the work he was obviously born to do, in her estimation, and no matter what happened in their relationship, she would support whatever he decided to do.

Todd knew she was right. He'd been at it to the long to up and quit when things started to get rough.

He said goodbye to the kids and their grandmother, kissed Brighty goodbye, and left. Back at the office a couple of days later, he learned that Jim would be arriving that day from Jamaica and made preparations to have a helicopter take them north to the site where the fugitives' ambulance had been located.

The helicopter flew them over the countryside alive with the colors of fall. It was late in the afternoon when they landed in the deep ravine where there was a crisp chill in the air, far different from the warm weather still prevailing in D.C. It was the day after the ambulance had been discovered.

Jim breathed in the smell of wildflowers as he and Todd walked towards the ambulance.

There were already units from the D.C. task force set up to handle the manhunt that Todd and Jim were now in charge of.

Jim noticed someone had already bought in a couple of local bloodhounds and were scouting a nearby cornfield that had recently been leveled to try and pick up the trail of the fugitives. They were being given all the latest information as they inspected the vehicle, when one of the Pennsylvania state troopers reported that the dogs seem to have found something.

They hurried out to the field where the dogs began to howl and growl, pulling on their leashes in the direction of a small stand of trees.

The trooper holding the dogs unleash them. The three dogs ran off howling towards the trees.

On the ground, the earth was soaked with what looked like blood. Jim knelt down to take a closer look and confirmed that it was indeed blood. He got back on his feet looking in the direction of the stand of trees.

He began to follow along behind with Todd and the rest of the officers, some of whom carried shotguns.

Jim noticed the dogs had stopped barking when they entered the stand of trees. He hurried along and was one of the first to reach the trees. As he entered the stand, the darkness assailed him, and he immediately understood the reason why the trees were there in the first place.

He found the ground underneath transformed from terra firma to a swampish bog fed by a deep underground spring that sucked at his feet and threatened to pull his shoes off.

The farmers who had cleared the cornfield so many years ago had simply skirted the area of the bog and left the trees standing there as a visual reminder. As he moved deeper into the trees, he could hear the dogs mewing and sniffing just ahead of him.

He came upon a grisly sight. There were four headless bodies in the middle of the bog. One had been stripped of clothing and was lying chest down, but the other three, for some reason, were propped up with their backs against trees. It was a strange and foreboding sight and one that all who was there would remember for the rest of their lives.

Todd, who was just behind Jim, had lost one of his shoes trying to make his way through the muck and held it in his hand as he sidled up to his partner. He, too, was immediately mesmerized by the scene before him and stood there for quite some while his foot and pants cuff got soaked as he tried without success to make sense of the spectacle before them. This was definitely one for the books.

What happened to the heads? he wondered.

It seemed to him that this guy Franz Zimmerman was not normal by any standards, and he was beginning to believe maybe he wasn't very human either. He said to Jim, "Well I guess I've just about seen it all."

"Yeah, me too," retorted said Jim. "We got to get this guy back in custody as soon as possible, cause I got a feeling things could get a whole lot worse from now on if we don't!"

As they began to examine the crime scene, two hundred miles to the north Franz and Adrian were driving by way of back roads to a destination that would take them through eight states.

The task force had no idea where they were headed, but there was someone who did. Someone who had decided to do something about it.

Earlier the ambulance had been making its way to the trauma center. The night sky was filled with the clouds and approaching rainstorm.

Inside the moving vehicle, Adrian opened his eyes.
The young prison doctor asked Adrian how he was
doing and in a whisper he said his mouth was dry. The
doctor told him they were getting to a hospital in about
half an hour and proceeded to give him some water
from a canister.

Outside the rain started to fall. Pretty soon there
was a virtual downpour and the guard driving found he
had to slow down because of poor visibility. Up ahead,
a car had spun around on the slick road. The guard
jammed on his brakes, sending S3's head into the
partition separating the front of the vehicle from the
rear.

S3 slumped momentarily unconscious to the floor.

The guard and the doctor in the rear were shaken
up a little, but otherwise they were okay, as the vehicle
started to move again.

Once the vehicle had stopped, the guard riding
shotgun opened a partition and asked if everyone was
all right and if they needed any help. He watched the
two men in back trying to lift S3 off the cramped floor.

They said they could manage and closed the
partition door. The guard found it difficult to maneuver
S3, with his arm shackled behind his back, took his
keys from his belt and removed the cuffs from S3's
hands.

They were able to get S3 up on the bench and the
doctor knelt on his knees, checking for dilation of S3's
eye with a small penlight. As the guard started to re-
cuff S3's hands, S3 made his move.

With his free hands, he grabbed both men by the
throat and squeezed. His grip was like an iron vice and
in the moments that followed both men struggled to
pull away, but too soon their wind pipes were crushed

like pieces of paper and crumpled to the floor where life deserted them.

S3 retrieve the guard's keys and gun. Soon he had his leg irons free as Adrian looked on in horror.

S3 stood up smiling down at Adrian and silenced him with a finger to his lips as he knocked on the partition.

When the guard opened the door, S3 shot him in the forehead and pointed the gun at the driver, telling him to take the next turn. The driver did as he was told and soon they found themselves far away from the city in a rural area where S3 finally had the driver pull over. He subsequently shot the man in the head. He put both bodies in .the back of the ambulance, with Adrian, before getting in the driver's seat, heading north.

A strange thing had happened to Franz Zimmerman when he was momentarily unconscious. Psychologically speaking, you might say that when he came to, his alter ego was in control and the Franz Zimmerman the world once knew, never again regained consciousness. For all intents and purposes he had ceased to exist that fateful moment, when his head struck the partition of the ambulance.

Hans was running the show now, and it was Hans who drove north for hours, until he reached Lancaster County, northwest of the city of brotherly love, Philadelphia. There he pulled the ambulance over to the side of the road and went into the back choosing a dead guard with the same physical makeup as himself - and removed the man's uniform, setting it aside.

Adrian watched in morbid fascination as S3 began to drag each body from the rear of the vehicle, but couldn't see him as he continued to drag each one out into the night across the deserted road to the middle of a cornfield, where he methodically severed each head with a scalpel and put each one in a plastic bag he'd taken from the ambulance. He dragged the bodies from that spot to a clump of trees not too far from where he severed the heads and hid them from view.

When he was finally finished, he donned the guard's uniform he'd chosen for himself and got inside the ambulance, closing the door behind him.

He greeted Adrian, *"Guten Abend."*

Adrian gasped. He now knew who this monster was.

Trying to compose himself he replied, "Franz, I thought you were still back in prison. You've changed so much I... I didn't recognize you until now." He gulped as he laid strapped to the bed staring into that horrible visage and continued; "I... I'm sorry about not being able to help you, but you know it was for the protection of everyone that I couldn't risk taking the chance." Adrian tried to bluster.

"I'm sure that you, as well as anyone, knows the price we all would have paid, though in retrospect I guess it really doesn't matter now, does it? The only thing that matters is we're free now and we must make a plan."

Hans replied, "Your friend Franz is no longer with us." He began to untie Adrian. He lifted the man and sat him on the bench much to Adrian's discomfort.

He had been very lucky, his stabs wounds in reality had been minor, thanks to the fact the screwdriver wielded by Ruiz Alvarez, cleanly missed all the major organs and with the exception of a case of peritonitis, he'd escaped severe injury. But none the less, the pain from the two stab wounds was enough to make him very uncomfortable whenever he moved.

He wondered what it was S3 had meant, when from outside the ambulance, a car could be heard approaching and then stopping. A car door opened and closed as S3 switched off the interior light, and in a few moments there was a knock at the back of the door as two voices could be heard arguing whether or not to open the vehicle up.

The door handle finally turned and it was at that moment with a great roar S3 slammed into the opening door and attacked the two stunned young men who'd fallen to the ground.

They never stood a chance as S3 took their lives in a moment of violent chaos that came and went like a deadly squall in the night.

He took the two bodies and put them in the back of the jeep the men had been driving, to dispose of later and got Adrian out of the ambulance. S3 put him in the passenger seat of the jeep along with the trash bag of severed heads, which made Adrian very uncomfortable, because it leaked a lot of blood.

S3 also took the doctor's case and filled it with numerous items from the ambulance before finally getting into the driver's side of the jeep and continued northward leaving the ambulance behind in the dead of night. He drove about three miles before stopping on a wooden bridge to remove the two bodies from the jeep.

He dragged them down under the bridge one by one, where he cut off their heads and put them in another trash bag. Returning to the jeep, he found that Adrian was beginning to moan and groan from the pain he was suffering, and S3 reached inside of the doctor's case removing one of the Durelgesic pads.

These pads were used to help comfort cancer patients and had a heroine-like affect that usually lasted up to three days. He peeled off the wrapper and stuck the pad on Adrian's exposed arm.

Adrian was still wearing his hospital gown and S3 covered him with one of the blankets he'd retrieved from the ambulance before he continued on his journey. He had a special reason for wanting to keep Adrian alive, a very special reason indeed.

CHAPTER 23

Jennifer worried her mother about letting her visit Aunt Beatrice in Canada every day they remained in Jamaica. And though Beverly didn't know at the time why the girl seemed to be so possessed with the idea, she soon relented and made the arrangements for her daughter to leave that very weekend. After all, it might do her some good to get away and be independent for a while.

In British Columbia, there would be a private tutor to keep Jennifer on top of her studies and a car and driver to take her around, if that's what she wanted to do.

Beverly would be returning to Connecticut at the same time to await Jim's return to New Haven. The investigators, who had eventually found the counterfeit money that Adrian and his thugs buried on the premises of the estate, were gone and it was time to close down the villa until she or Jim decided that they were ready to use it again.

She knew she would miss her daughter, but felt compelled to give the girl, who seemed so much more like a young woman now, some space.

So a few days later they said goodbye to each other at Montego Bay International Airport and boarded separate planes.

Beverly flew into Kennedy Airport New York and Jennifer was bound for British Columbia via Boston Massachusetts and Montreal. It was best that Jennifer disappeared. She would later confess that she got off the plane in Boston and passed through customs before leaving the airport.

The day of the disappearance, Beverly did receive a call from her daughter who let her know that she was fine and told her not to worry.

She said there was something she had to do for Jim and no matter how much Beverly begged and pleaded, the girl refused to give in and tell her mother where she was. She said she would call back in a couple of days and after telling her mother she loved her, she hung up.

Beverly was upset, but something inside of her told her that Jennifer would be all right. So she prayed for her daughter and hoped for the best. It was all she could do for now.

When Jennifer left the airport she took a cab to downtown Boston and using her mother's platinum American Express credit card she secreted away in Jamaica. She called a local hotel and reserved a room.

When she got to the hotel they told her they couldn't let a twelve-year-old girl check-in until she told the woman at reservations that her mom and dad were held up at the airport because all their baggage had been lost and they had sent her ahead because she wasn't feeling well. Could she at least please go up to her room and lie down?

The woman turned the problem over to the manager who allowed Jennifer to sign the register since the credit had already been established and they had all the pertinent information.

He told her that he hoped her parents found their luggage and rang for a bellboy to take her up to the room.

She was taken up to the tenth floor and ushered into a room where as soon as the bellboy left, she called home and talked to her mother.

She knew she had a couple of days at best before they found her there, so she devised a plan which would enable her to sidetrack anyone who might come looking for her.

That day she enjoyed the comforts of the room and ordered up a dinner insisting of a gigantic steak burger with French fries and a milkshake while she watched one of the latest movies on the pay per view service.

After a good night's sleep she gathered her few belongings, and leaving the hotel, set out for Beacon Hill and the Commons.

There she found a family on a Saturday picnic and told them a story about being a runaway pursued by an Italian pimp who was looking for her but didn't know where she was. She said she was afraid to go to the police because of what might happen to her if the pimp found out.

The woman immediately took pity on the seemingly forlorn young woman and invited her to stay with them until she was able to get her life back in order.

Jennifer readily accepted the offer and joined the family for the rest of the day's activities and went with them to their home. That evening she called her mother again and talked for a while before promising to call the next day.

She was given a sofa bed to sleep on and that night she had a dream.

In her dream there was the one eyed demon, and it was looking for her but couldn't see her yet. There was something that was blocking the Cyclops view of her, and she was glad for it because she knew that if it could see her it would quickly learn what it was she was up to and would stop whatever it was doing and seek to destroy her. She was safe for now. The important thing was she could sense in her dream where the Cyclops was headed and what it was doing. She also knew that this was the very reason it looked for her. But tonight she would get the shock of her life because for the first time it spoke to her.

As if from a dark void the voice came to her in the dream; "Who... Are... You?

In her sleep Jennifer tried to wake up but the voice held her in its dark grip. "Why... do... you... seek... Me...?"

Its one eye seemed to grow as it turned this way and that way, striving to find her. Her body tossed and turned in an effort to hide from the terrible being, and she was sure it was about to see her when a curtain seemed to close between her and Cyclops. The demon bellowed in anger and tried to rend the curtain, but Jennifer used all her will to help keep the curtain in place. It was a supreme moment and one that would hold her well in the future. When she awoke the sheets on the bed were soaked with sweat, and she knew it was time to tell Jim what she had learned in the dream.

She called home that morning and asked her mother to reach Jim and tell him to meet her in two days in Acadia, Maine, at the Greyhound bus terminal.

Beverly was ecstatic that her daughter had decided to put an end to her journey and told her she would be there to meet her.

But Jennifer said that it was important that she stayed home. It was just too dangerous and it was something that only she and Jim could do. Beverly became angry and tried to get the young woman to allow her to be there also, but Jennifer steadfastly refused.

At last, Beverly accepted her terms glad just to get her daughter back home anyway she could. When they hung up she called Jim and told him about the call from Jennifer and Jim said he would be glad to go get the girl if that's the way she wanted it.

When Jennifer hung up the phone from making her reservation with Greyhound, she was a little exasperated at her mother's insistency. *Mothers were always like that, quick to become angry at the littlest things.*

She made up her mind right then and there that when she became a mother she would be more understanding of her children's needs.

She joined her surrogate family for Sunday breakfast and told them that she'd worked things out over the phone with her own family and would be taking the bus home tomorrow, thanking them for their kindness. The family was very happy for her and offered to take her to the bus station the following day. She accepted the offer expressing her gratitude the best she could.

That night again, she dreamed of Cyclops, but this time it was safely kept at a distance behind the curtain which seemed to follow it where ever it went and it couldn't tell she was there at all.

It was as if she could peek around the edge of the curtain and watch the demon as it walked down a road of fire and set fire to signposts all along the way. At one point it stopped and turned looking in her direction, but she ducked behind the curtain and he turned and continued on his way. In his hand he carried a huge hammer that occasionally he would use on some poor soul.

It was at once frightening and fascinating as she looked into the demon's hell, and she was beginning to comprehend the demon's ultimate purpose.

It was on a quest to take the lives of as many poor souls as it could and in causing it seemed to find joy in being.

In reality it kept the heads of its victims as keepsakes and reminders of the beauty of death, true deadheads.

When she awoke the next morning there was urgency about her and she couldn't wait to get started. On the way to the bus station, the car they were riding in suffered a flat tire and since they were not well to do as a family, the father never had enough money to own a spare. There was very little she could do to help. So after thanking the kind people once more she hailed a cab and left them stranded in the middle of the street.

Two weeks later, the family would wake up and find a brand new Lincoln town car parked in their driveway. A huge red ribbon was tied to it with titles and keys plus a two year fully paid insurance policy in the mail slot. There was a thank you note from Jennifer, Beverly and Jim to the people would open their hearts and home to a stranger who once needed their help.

When Jennifer got to the bus station, she picked up her ticket and boarded the bus for Acadia. The ride took more than twelve hours, and when she got there it was two in the morning and she had nowhere to go in the sleeping town. The weather had changed dramatically and she put on one of the coats she had brought with her all the way from Jamaica as she walked the streets of the city.

She returned to the station where she fell asleep on one of the stations benches. When she woke up she was startled to find that it was daytime and the station was bustling with activity. She went to the cafeteria and sat down at one of the booths and ordered breakfast.

Halfway through her meal she saw someone standing before her and looked up to see Jim smiling down at her. She jumped up, hugged him tightly, and he said, "Now what's this all about, Jennifer? Running away and everything?"

They sat back down in the booth, and Jennifer said, "Jim, I think know where they're going, but I have to be there when you find them."

"Why Jennifer?"

"Because I know that it's the only way for us to stop him. You and me together, I mean."

"Jennifer," Jim said exasperated. "You've got to understand that I just can't go and risk your life. If something were to happen to you, I could never forgive myself."

"If I can tell you something that will make your boss believe me, then can I stay with you until you find them? Because if you don't I'll just run away again." Jennifer was very serious and Jim knew it.

There was something different about her now, and Jim thought for a moment before getting up and walking over to a group of officers who'd accompanied him to the bus station. One of them went outside and returned shortly with a cell phone.

Jim returned to the booth and sat back down. He made a call on the phone and talked for a moment before handing the phone over to Jennifer. At first she thought it was her mother on the other end and was a little perturbed until she realized that she was talking to someone who must have been Jim's boss.

Jim told her to tell him what it was she wanted to do and to give him some information if she could.

Jennifer did as she was told and mentioned that they could find four bodies in some trees near a hospital truck and two more bodies under a bridge before handing the phone back to Jim.

Todd, who was on the other end, told Jim he would get back to them once he checked out her information.

They all left the bus station and went to the local police station where they waited for Todd to call back.

While they waited he called Beverly and put Jennifer on the line, who told her mother again not to worry and that she would be home soon.

Jim took the phone and explained to Beverly what had happened. If Jennifer's psychic information turned out to be correct Jim said it would be helpful if she remained to help them capture the two fugitives once and for all.

Beverly replied if it would finally put an end to things and if Jennifer could be with her most of the time, then it was fine by her, if that's what Jennifer wanted to do.

Jim said "great" and told Jennifer the news.

It was just turning dark when Todd finally called back and told Jim that they had found two bodies under a bridge about three 'miles from where the ambulance had originally been found.

It was a great revelation, and the officers there at the station found themselves looking at Jennifer with new respect.

There was something unsettling about having an honest-to-God psychic in their midst. And Jennifer was a psychic whose powers would mean the difference between life and death for millions of people.

Jim, at some point, asked her why she had come to Maine. She told everyone in the room that the two fugitives were on their way to this particular town, and they would have to hurry if they were going to catch them before they disappeared into the forest.

An all-points bulletin was issued, and the task force was flown in and set up in the town hall of Acadia. Citizens were warned not to talk to or pick up strangers and to keep their doors and windows locked at all times. Pictures of both men were carried on all the news channels, and a dragnet, including blockades and car checks, was set up to intercept the two fugitives.

Finally on the third day, a Jeep ran one of the car check points and pursuit was given, but the vehicle was lost in the vicinity of Acadia National Park. Since the park itself covered more than 1000 square miles, the National Guard was called in to assist in the search.

For the next three weeks the task force searched the woods and forest for the two men in vain. And then the winter storm-of-the-season moved into the area. As the first snows began to fall, it became increasingly difficult to continue the search without more help and supplies, so the search was temporarily called off until the snow let up.

Meanwhile unbeknownst to the task force, the two fugitives were no longer in Arcadia. Instead they were keeping warm at a deserted ranger's station fifty miles away in another park known as Finger Lakes National Reserve and area that also contained the Finger Lakes Nuclear Power Plant.

For years, due to its proximity and easy access, Finger Lakes was considered to be a prime location for a major terroristic attack on U.S. soil by the various terrorist groups around the world, though no one had made serious effort concerning the facility.

They had reached the station after a long torturous drive through the woods and immediately made the cabin habitable.

Long ago, S3 got his training at this very area for the Palestinian Homeland Army and knew the station was there. He was surprised to find it deserted as he approached the cabin through the woods on foot that first day. The building was filled with the necessities for survival in the wilderness, such as a store of canned and dry foods, assorted axes and knives, and two cots with folded blankets next to a large potbellied stove.

The station also contained three oil lamps with a five gallon oil drum. The same evening the snow began to fall, S3 had a fire going and Adrian was asleep in one of the cots. Over the next two weeks, S3 chopped wood and scouted the power plant nearby as Adrian's health deteriorated.

S3 also devised a plan to enter the well-guarded facility and was prepared to make his move within the next few days, but there was something he had to do first.

Over the next couple of days, the storm had literally buried the town of Bangor and surrounding villages and roadways in the vicinity, under more than three feet of snow, with drifts as high as eight feet.

It was one of the worst storms to hit Maine in over 20 years. The National Weather Service was warning of at least another week of snow and Jim decided it was time for Jennifer to go home.

She'd been in Arcadia for close to three weeks and with the exception of foreseeing the arrival in the area of the two fugitives, she had not been able to contribute any more information. But Jennifer refused to leave, saying it was almost time for Cyclops to make his move.

With the weather being so poor, Jim relented and told her she could stay until the snow ended, after that she was going home. Jennifer agreed.

She busied herself in the coming days by helping the local Red Cross, who had set up shop in the high school gym for stranded travelers and anyone else who needed shelter from the storm and something hot to eat. There were blankets and hot chocolate to hand out, along with emergency medical care for hypothermia and frostbite.

And there was growing admiration among the volunteers for the little lady who strove tirelessly to give comfort to those who needed it.

She often went back to the hotel, exhausted, and it was during one of those nights that she had her most important dream of all.

In the dream, she saw Cyclops standing in the middle of a hand, who's fingers were made out of water. It was looking over a huge array of electronic equipment and in its hand, it raised the hammer it always seem to be carrying and began to strike equipment, causing a great explosion, releasing a poison in the air. It spread across the land killing all life as far away as New York.

The next morning she called Jim and told him about the dream, and he called an emergency meeting of the task force where Jennifer was able to recount her dream in full.

Afterwards, someone mentioned that the hand with fingers of water could very well mean that the fugitives were up at the Finger Lake reserve, which was quit near a nuclear plant of the same name. The silence in the room was scary. No one had thought to consider the possibility that the nuclear plant could be in danger.

Jim told someone to get on the horn and warn the plant to beef up security. A few minutes later it was announced that the nuclear facility did not answer, though someone raised the idea that the lines to the plant could be out due to storm. But Jim was sure that was not the case. He dispatched two detachments of men, one to check out the plant and one to check out any possible habitats within the park. He also called Todd Morrison and asked him to fly out from Washington as quick as possible.

Todd knew the roads past Boston were all snowed and in a commercial flight would be of no help to him, but he was able to get a National Guard jet to fly in from Andrews Air Force Base to Bangor.

He arrived in Arcadia's town hall within four hours of talking Jim on the phone. It seemed that no sooner had Todd arrived, Jim started receiving reports from the field.

The detachments found the going rough and heavy falling snow with drifts sometimes reach above their heads, but were able to make headway with the help of snow cats and skis. One of the first places the park detachment checked was the ranger station.

They approached the cabin with stealth, but did not meet with any resistance as they entered the building.

Inside they found the cabin well lived in, and they also found two bags full of severed heads, which they took. It seemed the two fugitives once again slipped away. At the power plant, another detachment found two guards at the front gate dead from bullet wounds and upon reaching Entrance Four discovered more dead bodies outside of the huge concrete door, which was now sealed from the inside and impossible to open.

Jim was told that Entrance Four was the location by which all workers entered and departed the plant. This was pertinent, because just inside there was a special area containing facilities for checking radiation levels and showers for departing workers. Somehow the fugitives must've gone by security and set off interior alarms which automatically shut the concrete door, sealing the plant from the outside world.

A world that was now intent on finding out just what was going on inside and on the verge of mass hysteria in just a few more hours.

CHAPTER 24

Finger Lakes nuclear power plant was the crowning glory of Maine's nuclear fission program and was capable of supplying over six counties with electricity. It also had the distinction of being the only nuclear plant in the U.S. that had never once been cited by the Nuclear Regulatory Commission for any infraction of the NRC code.

Its capable senior director, Ron Kerber, had been proud of this fact for many years, but right now the NRC was the least of his worries. For before him stood a vision straight out of hell, brandishing a semi-automatic rifle in his direction.

He had been one of the first to respond to the central alarm coming from Entrance Four and had run from his office to try and find out what the problem was, when his ears had been assaulted with the sounds of multiple gun shots coming directly from the direction in which he was running.

He tried to stop and reverse direction, but before he could, S3 came in to view just ahead of him near the radiation detectors. It was all he could do to keep from screaming out at the horror he saw before him. The bodies of plant workers and security guards lay scattered on the floor as others tried to hide from S3 behind some of the huge generators just inside Entrance Four.

Moaning and crying came from some of the survivors and a few brave souls were trying to help the wounded heedless of the danger to themselves. To Senior Director Ron Kerber, it was like a scene out of Dante's Inferno, and he began to hope it was a dream that he would soon wake up from.

S3 had spotted him though and somehow guessed that he was important to his plans, so he leveled his rifle at the man, gesturing for him to approach carefully.

Ron did as he was told and soon found himself standing in front of a vision straight out of hell. The vision was holding a man by the scruff of the neck, but Ron had no idea who the man was.

Beside him huddled on the floor and on the verge of collapse, was Adrian Perez. Adrian had been more or less dragged around that day by S3 and as the senior director approached S3 released his hold on the exhausted man who fell back on the floor, his head making a loud cracking sound as it hit the concrete tiles.

S3 looked at his prey and said, "You will show me the way to the containment chambers. Ya?"

Ron Kerber was nobody's fool. He immediately sensed that this monster was capable of doing a great deal of harm to a great many people, and he had no intentions whatsoever of leading the man to the most dangerous area of the plant.

He turned around and was headed in the opposite direction of where S3 wanted to go when he heard a loud gunshot and simultaneously felt something slam into his right shoulder.

He was knocked to the ground by the impact of the bullet and was slow to get to his feet. Realizing he'd just been shot, he figured that the man must know where the containment chambers were located.

"You must not play games with me," S3 said. "I am aware of which direction we must proceed, so I will advise you not to go the wrong direction again."

Ron's fear was great. He could not do what this man was asking of him and yet seemingly he had no other choice. Blood ran down the front of his chest, and he held his left hand over the wound.

He turned and started off in the right direction. In a few minutes they reached the first chamber which was sealed by a radioactive proof system of coated steel doors. Just inside the first door was where workers donned protective outfits, reminiscent of NASA spacesuit, in order to work inside the chamber, and the door beyond that led to the containment chamber itself.

S3 directed the man to open the first door, and this time Ron did as he was told. He punched in a sequence of numbers on the code bar next to the door, and a few seconds later the door automatically swung open.

S3 slammed the butt of his rifle against the back of Ron's head, knocking him unconscious and stepped into the outer chamber as the door slowly closed behind him.

He did not bother to don one of the suits and instead walked over to the second steel door. The square button which caused the door to slide open, and he stepped into the containment chamber where he found himself looking over a railing that was about 100 feet above a huge vat filled with clear water emanating a strange blue light from huge rods in the middle of it all.

S3 knew he was looking in the face of radioactive death, and he reveled in the feeling that was beginning to wash over him. He knew that time was of the essence and from around his waist he removed four grenades he'd taken from the guard, shack out in front of the plant and placed them on the steel deck underneath him. Quietly, he stripped his clothes from his body and awaited the night.

Outside the chamber Ron Kerber had regained consciousness and had made his way to the main control room of the facility where most of the other survivors of S3's attack had congregated.

One of the first people he saw was his assistant, Daye Garner, who ran over to him saying, "Boss! We thought you were dead!" He led Ron to a seat at the main terminal console and proceeded to administer to Ron's bullet wound.

As Ron gazed at the readouts on the big board before him, he asked, "What is the status of the containment chambers?"

"Everything looks normal and the emergency shutdown is still in effect so all generators are quiet, but our terrorist or whoever the hell he is, has somehow gained entry into containment chamber number three, and god help us if he somehow meddles with the temperatures in there.

"Who is he and how the hell did he get in here?"

"I wish I knew... I wish I knew."

Dave had finished patching up his shoulder, the best he could, so Ron stood up from his seat and turned to face the people in the room.

"Listen up everyone..." He waited until he made sure he had everybody's attention and then continued. "We have a code six here as I am sure most of you are all aware. But for those who aren't I would like to try and explain what has happened.

It seems that about two hours ago, a terrorist made his way into this facility, killing and wounding a number of people in the process. And to make things worse, he has gained entry to one of the containment chambers."

There was frantic murmuring among the employees in the room, and Ron had to raise his voice in order to regain their attention.

"There will be nothing gained if we all start to panic. Now please everyone, just settle down."

When everyone was quiet he said, "You will all don radiation suits and evacuate the facility immediately. And I am sure that by now the proper authorities will be waiting for you once you get outside."

He turned to Dave and said, "You proceed with the evacuation and get everyone out of here."

"But what about you boss?"

"Someone has to remain here to monitor what is going on in that containment chamber, and that job is mine and mine alone. Now get going."

Ron turned his back on his assistant and sat back down at the main console.

Dave hurriedly began to usher the employees out of the control room to the emergency evacuation point located just outside the room where there were plenty of radiation suits for everyone. There was a feeling of dread among the people there as they began to put on their suits.

It was anyone's guess what awaited them once they began to make their way back to the entrance and most wondered if they would live through the ordeal.

Once outside of Entrance Four, the task force had to set up a command post and had started to evacuate the area of all residents and tourists for a hundred miles in every direction. Jim and Todd waited inside a trailer that had been provided by the National Guard that was being used as a communication center. Jennifer Perez was also there.

She had proved herself invaluable, and Jim knew that the difference between failure and success depended a lot upon information she could possibly provide the task force about what was going on inside the nuclear facility.

Night had finally fallen as the great door to Entrance Four swung open to allow the frightened employees to scurry out into the darkness and into the waiting hands of the National Guard, which the Governor of Maine had sent in once it became clear that there had been an attack on the Finger Lake Nuclear Facility.

Ron Kerber had opened the door to Entrance Four from the terminal console by using the facilities main computer to override the automatic lockdown command.

He was, for all intents and purposes, in control of the facility.

He was also in contact, by phone, with the attack force outside and by now everyone knew that S3 was inside one of the most dangerous areas of the facility and that he was armed. Unknown to Todd and Jim, the National Guard squad had put on the same radiation suits that the employees had worn and were awaiting the go ahead from the Colonel to enter the facility with the purpose of hunting down and killing the terrorist inside. Inside the command trailer, Jim, who was in charge of the entire operation, conferred with Jennifer for a moment and then spoke to the Colonel in charge of the National Guard.

"Colonel, my orders are to take this man alive if at all possible, and if he survives the radiation chamber, to return him to D.C. Now I know the threat of a meltdown is preeminent in everyone's mind, but, he began to smile, "my experts tell me that there is a way to remove him from the plant without any harm to the facility what so ever."

"Well, I sure in hell would like to know who these so called goddamn experts are!" the Colonel retorted.

"Now I know that some big wheels down there in Washington may have put you in charge up here, but personally, he prefaced by poking Jim in the chest with his index finger, "I don't think you know jack shit about what's going on here mister. My troops are poised to find that son of a bitch in there and kill him, and that's what were gonna' do. So just get out of my way."

"Colonel, I am now giving you a direct order," Jim said, looking the man squarely in the eye. "I want you to stand down your men until I direct you otherwise, and I want you to do it now! Is that understood?"

The silence in the trailer was palpable, but sensing that maybe he had overplayed his hand, the Colonel said, "Alright. Let's just see what your experts come up with... I'll give you just one hour and then we're goin' in!" He turned and left the trailer much to everyone's relief.

Jim turned to Todd wearily and said, "Jennifer thinks that there's a way to draw him out to us, and if she's right, we'll be able to trap him outside the plant... But it is a very dangerous proposition, and I'm not sure just how much help we can be to her."

Todd's face showed a look of horror as he replied, "What the hell do you mean, Jim? Certainly you're not thinking of letting that girl go in there, are you?"

"Oh no! It's nothing as dangerous as that, but... this time I think we will need your help," he replied with a smile.

And the three of them sat down amidst the turmoil inside the trailer to confer, as dark clouds overhead threatened to create one more problem for them, and maybe the world, in the deepening night.

CHAPTER 25

Adrian Perez was close to death, and he knew it.

Like everyone else, he knew that one day he would die but he was not ready for it.

For in death, he now realized that a terrible judgment would be made for all of the crimes he committed in life, and now he feared the retribution waiting for him. And he had every right to be afraid.

As he lay on the floor of the nuclear plant where all seemed to be so quiet. His life's blood seeped from a crack in his skull he received when S3 dumped him unceremoniously on the floor. The blood was creating a pool of dark fluid that held no reflection of life.

He tried to cry out for help, but at last the words would not come, and his final thought was of his dead mother who momentarily seemed to be standing before him with her arms held out reaching for him, before turning her back and retreating into a light in which he would not be able to follow.

Then... Adrian Perez was no more.

Inside the radiation chamber, S3 had been laying for hours in a trance-like state as the radiation washed over and through him. His skin had begun to flake and peel as blood seeped from his ears and nose. But suddenly he was awakened by a vision. He sat up and smiled, his one eye searching here and there for the source of the vision.

Outside under the flood lights, directly in front of Entrance Four, Jim, Todd, and Jennifer stood with their hands linked together in the swirling snow as Jennifer focused her mind upon the Cyclops. Immediately she could feel that he had found them. Inside the plant, S3 stood up and faced in the direction of the entrance.

"Ha ha ha... So! It is you again! And this time it seems you have company."

Jennifer heard the words in her mind, and they felt like the blows of a hammer. She screamed out in pain, though to her astonishment, she sensed that Jim and Todd were experiencing the same pain as she was.

This fact seemed to give her the strength she needed to continue. Mentally she said, "Yes, Yes, I'm here."

"Foolish of you *mein Freulein*. For you, your friends, and many, many others will end up just as your father did only a few moments ago."

Jennifer suddenly saw a mental picture of her father being repeatedly torn apart by many horrible visages. And for a second, it seemed as if he could see her somehow, and she thought she heard the words... "forgive me."

But quickly the vision dissipated. Jennifer was undaunted.

"I'm not afraid of you. You're nothing but a big bully and a coward. And if you weren't hiding in there like a scared rabbit you'd come out here and face me so I could kick you for all the things you've done to my family."

Jennifer smiled and said, "And besides... You're not a real demon after all, are you? You're just a real ugly man!""

Todd looked at Jim and smiled.

S3 suddenly bellowed in a psychic rage that knocked all three of them to their knees.

He was enraged by the disrespect accorded him by the girl and decided he could not allow such an affront. He kicked the door to the containment chamber off its hinges and walked through the second door which was still open it closed behind him earlier on his way to Entrance Four.

The nuclear plant would now have to wait, for he felt he needed to teach them what hell was all about. So he began to send a wave of mental energy that stunned everyone within a mile unconscious, except for Jim, Todd, and Jennifer

When he walked out of Entrance Four, there was no one there to stop him except for the three, he was seeing and they had recovered and were standing on their feet waiting for him as he approached.

CHAPTER 26

Thirty years previously in the small town of Milltown, Virginia, a small group of men and women led by a man named James Potter, banded together to worship the devil.

In their desire to show their faith and loyalty, they tried to raise from hell one of Lucifer's most terrible demons, Hansragoth, the one eyed cleaver of souls, known to the worshipers to be the one who would visit the most destruction upon the earth.

One winter's night they made their attempt and almost succeeded, almost. The demon only partially entered earth's plane, due to the group's inability to understand the ancient techniques necessary to accomplish such a dangerous feat though Hansragoth, in its wrath, was able to destroy the members of the group on hand and, embedded its evil in the leather jacket that James Potter wore that-night.

James Potter's grandson Aaron inherited the jacket when his grandmother died nearly twenty-eight years later.

Aaron had been a loving and devoted child to his parents and an honor student at St. Mary's High School in D.C. when he received the jacket in a box from his father.

That night he was to go bowling with some friends and decided to wear the jacket which he thought was kind of neat since he had never owned anything that had been made of leather before. That night was to mark a change in him that would bewilder his parents and everyone who knew him. As the weeks went by, they would see him join a group of skinheads prone to violence and become involved in skirmishes with the police.

Ultimately, he dropped out of school and became the leader of the gang. Guiding them in evermore violent activities, for little did he or anyone else know that the leather jacket he wore religiously everyday was, in fact, a portal by which Hansragoth was strengthening his hold on earth's plane.

But it was not until Franz Zimmerman and Aaron Potter encountered each other that fateful day on the subway that Hansragoth realized the medium by which he could truly enter the earth's plane. The medium by which it could ultimately destroy the earth and allow his master to finally rule in triumph.

And though Aaron Potter had turned in the right direction he was not completely evil. And it was complete, uncompromising evil that Hansragoth needed. S3 was completely evil.

That day on the subway, Hansragoth called to S3, commanding him to take the jacket from Aaron and the rest shall we say is history.

Hansragoth was able to possess S3's body, sending his soul to hell, and it was Hansragoth, the cleaver of souls, that the three companions, Jim, Jennifer, and Todd now faced and faced alone or so they thought.

In reality, there would actually be four to face the mighty demon that night.

In the darkness of the night, Jamal Walker's SUV made its way through the fallen snow up the road to Finger Lakes National Park. It had been over a year since he had single handedly captured the most dangerous killer the world had ever seen in one Franz Zimmerman, and so much had changed since then.

First, he had successfully gone through a three month drug rehabilitation program and afterwards moved in with his wife, the mother of his two children. Unbelievably, he had also done well in the business world. He invested $50,000 of the $100,000 dollar reward money he'd received in his stepfather's dry cleaning business which allowed them to open three new laundries. A few weeks later ,capitalizing on his fame and notoriety, he competed for and subsequently won a Government contract to clean the uniforms of all blue collar employees of the National Park Service in the D.C. area.

Every day, their three cleaning trucks, which now carried the name of "Woods and Walker Dry Cleaning Specialists" on the side, picked up and delivered over a thousand uniforms at various locations.

And at five dollars a pop, he had taken a business that was barely clearing five hundred a week and turned it around to earnings that would break the million dollar mark within a year. Yes. Things had certainly changed.

He smiled at himself for a moment, realizing that even the jeep he had driven all the way from D. C. had been leased for him by his accountants as a necessary business deduction.

Yes, things had been going very well, until, that is, the dreams started.

At first... they seemed meaningless. Just what seemed to be a few wild dreams of that crazy Franz Zimmerman. He thought that maybe it was due in part to possible brain damage resulting from his former drug use, but when he started to visualize other people who seemed to be reaching out for him, he instinctively knew that there was something far more to it than that.

He slowly began to realize that he had been having these dreams all along, but because he had been using drugs, he had failed to remember them and early on, it dawned on him that his coming into contact with Franz Zimmerman could not have merely been a coincidence.

And then just two weeks before, he read an article about Jennifer and Beverly Perez that also contained a picture of the two of them together in the paper and was stunned to recognize Jennifer. It was at that moment that he realized he'd been seeing her all along in his dreams.

That very same night, he began dreaming that this young lady was reaching out to him for help and the dreams each night after that became stronger and in more and more detail, until a few nights ago. That's when he finally learned what he felt was the truth, in one last horrifying dream and knew that he was desperately needed. He explained the situation to his wife and father in-law as clearly and as strongly as he could while expressing how important it was for him to see if it really all was just a dream or not.

Both Iris and her father were well aware of the nightmare Jennifer and Beverly Perez had experienced and though Jamal could not prove what he felt in his heart, they believed that he believed in what he was saying and that was good enough for the both of them. After he had put drugs behind him, he had shown them both ability beyond their wildest dreams. It was an ability to perceive things.

It was almost uncanny now the way he seemed to understand the beginning and the end of any given situation and correctly predict its outcome. He had more than once revealed this ability to them.

They reassured him that they were more than willing to support him in his journey all the way. There was one thing he didn't tell them about his dreams though and that was the part about Hansragoth. And it was with more than a little trepidation that he'd left home the previous day on his way to a place he'd only seen in his dreams. A place that held all the keys to the, mystery of his inner self. He knew that there was an important role for him to play somehow, someway in this obvious, (at least to him) battle of good versus evil. But the fear of the unknown can be a terrible thing. As Jamal drove on he glanced at the clock and saw that he was only a few minutes away from his final destination.

As the three companions stood where they were trying to gather their wits about them, S3 approached.

This is not going to be easy, Jim thought as he watched S3. He could feel the being radiate some kind of force or power that seemed to threaten to consume them.

When S3 was only a few feet away, he stopped and stood there, eying them casually, but remained silent and motionless.

Jim knew that the creature was mentally searching them out and he could feel the hairs on the back of his neck stand on end as S3's psychic fingers touched and probed around in his mind, seeking his strengths as well as his weaknesses.

Jennifer was the first to speak, for as soon as she had shaken off the effects of Hansragoth, first attack, her anger had grown stronger by the moment.

"I know who you are..." She spat, looking over at Jim and Todd. "He's not really who you think he is."

Todd queried, "What makes you say that?"

Jennifer turned to look back, at S3 and slowly she said, "Because I know who he really is now and where he comes from, too."

Hansragoth spoke, "Before the girl continues, let me say to you that she is absolutely correct in her powerful and gifted perception of the reality of the situation, gentlemen. So if you will... allow me to introduce myself."

At that moment, Hansragoth seemed to grow in front of their eyes, and his voice became as an echo through some distant mountain valley when he finally spoke again.

"I... am Hansragoth... Third claw of the master's hand, cleaver of souls and the precursor of this world's destruction. For many eons I have lived in the great black hole of fire from which no soul can escape and now... finally, I have come up to this world of mankind to prepare the way for the master of ultimate glory and rapture."

Todd looked at his two companions and said, "Do you believe this guy?"' He laughed aloud with as much bluster as he could manage.

"This guy's got more personalities than Sybil! Okay Hans, Magoo or whatever your name is... Be a good fellow and let us talk to Franz, okay?"

"Franz is... shall we say, acquainting himself with some of the lower environs of my master's world at the moment and is really quite unable to make an appearance here this evening."

Suddenly, car lights shone on the road leading to the entrance of the plant directly behind the three companions. Todd risked turning his head around and saw a four wheel drive rapidly approach, crunching the snow underneath its wheels as it came to a halt directly behind them.

Jamal got out of his vehicle and immediately recognized the two detectives from the death house and thought he knew the little girl from newspaper or TV reports. But there was no doubt as to whom they were facing.

He walked to the three companions, never taking his eyes off of Hansragoth.

Out of the corner of his mouth he said, "What's up with all these people lying around on the ground like they're dead or something?"

Hansragoth looked in his direction and smiled, then spoke with a droll tone of voice.

"Well! The gangs all here... How appropriate. Soooo... as they say... let the games begin."

And before anyone else could speak, he struck.

A bolt of psychic energy struck the four companions so hard it knocked them backwards off their feet, sending them dazed and sprawling into the snow, unable for the moment to move.

Hansragoth screamed in triumph and raised his head and fists to the sky shouting; "If this be the best this world can do to stop me... then prepare for the coming of the truly great warriors of hell. Chaos... Havoc... Hysteria... And Ruin!"

He turned and slowly started walking back to the entrance of the nuclear facility.

Jamal was the first to regain his feet and helped the others to theirs. He said, "Listen... I'm not quite sure why I'm here, but," he took a deep breath, "ever since the day I helped catch that crazy dude or whatever he is, I've been having these dreams, and they've just kept getting stronger and stronger until I had to get in my four wheel and drive up here like I did. What's up? It's like... like... I knew exactly where to come and everything!"

Jim looked at the retreating figure of Hansragoth and said, "I'm not sure anyone of us can answer that question, Mr. Walker, but there is one thing I do know now. And that is... somehow... we have been bought together here to stop this thing.

"I mean out of all the people in the world, for some reason it has been left up to the four of us to do what seems almost impossible to do, especially in the light of the powers that thing seems to possess." He paused, seemingly in deep thought and then continued.

"Nonetheless, the job has been given to us as you can see," he said looking around in the darkness. "No one else will be likely to join us in this thing." Jim fell silent as he again retreated into his own thoughts.

Todd spoke softly as he put his hands in his pockets in an effort to stay warm, "So... what should we be doing?" he said, "I mean, I think we're supposed to be doing something, right?"

Jamal looked up at the sky and asked, "Anybody got any ideas?"

The group was silent for a while as they all watched the retreating figure of Hansragoth.

Jennifer said, looking at the three adults, "Maybe we should pray to God, and he will help us. Me, my brother, and my mom used to hold hands and pray at night on the boat in Florida when we were about to go to sleep." She started to cry softly.

Jim put his arms around the little girl who suddenly seemed so young and vulnerable in the cold night, and said, "Well that sounds like as good a place to start as any."

The now solitary group of allies gathered around in a circle and with heads bowed, they clasped their hands together.

The effect was instantaneous and astounding.

From their center, a blue white fire seemed to erupt into the sky, fingering its way in short waves towards the nuclear facility where Hansragoth had almost reached the entrance.

The fire engulfed Hansragoth in a fist like embrace before he could enter the plant causing him to cry out in pain and rage.

With each wave, the fire seemed to get brighter and hotter until the demon Hansragoth turned and faced the group of defenders.

With great psychic focus, he was able to raise the fire slightly above his body and cast his own wave of energy at the body of warriors.

The energy struck them like a bolt of lightning, taking hold of their bodies and lifting them into the air.

But they were able to hold on to each other as they began to spin in a circle.

Jim cried out to his companions; "Don't let go! Whatever you do, hold on!'" The group began to spin so fast that it became a blur.

Hansragoth felt that it was now in control and sought to use its powers in even more devastating ways. It now began to focus energy towards the nuclear plant causing the ground beneath the building to tremble, but before he could cause any real damage, the hot fire started to drop back down around Hansragoth once again. He tried to re-focus his energies back to the spinning body of warriors, but now their power had become too strong, and the demon bellowed in a great rage as its earthly body was slowly consumed by the terrific short waves of flame until finally, it was no more than ashes in the wind.

The demon had never actually been able to enter the earth's plane and as the body of its host disintegrated, so did its very limited portal. But with the few moments it had left it was able to say as if in a tunnel far away, "Prepare thyself it is not overrrrrr..."

Then Hansragoth was gone.

The spinning group began to slow down and landed back on the ground on its feet. They were totally out of breath and everyone, with the exception of Jim, sank in exhaustion to the snow covered ground.

They looked at each other for a moment before Jim asked, "As long as everyone's all right, I'm not even going try and figure out what just happened here.'"

In the distance they could hear the voices of numerous people who were suddenly coming back to consciousness.

Some of the National Guard who had only moments before been lying on the ground in a deep coma like state, were now rushing up to the small group of warriors and upon seeing Jamal Walker, they raised their weapons threateningly.

But Todd Morrison, who had seen their approach, stepped in front of them, raising his hands shouting, "Don't even try it! This man's with us!"

Jennifer stood up and took Jamal's hand as he got to his feet and repeated, "He's with us." They smiled at each other. He spoke to Jennifer and said, "Hi! I'm Jamal Walker." Jennifer shook his hand and smiled saying, "I saw you on TV, Mr. Walker."

Jamal smiled and replied; "I saw you on TV, too."

But then his smile faded as he asked, "Now can someone please tell me am I dreaming all of this or what?"

At that moment the Colonel in charge of the National Guard came up to them in a huff and demanded to know what happened. The four combatants began to laugh, and Todd said, "Well, were not really sure what happened, but suffice it to say that the situation has been dealt with, and that the terrorist is now a pile of ashes."

The Colonel got right in Todd's face and shouted, "Well that don't quite make it, mister. I want to know what went on here, or I'll have you up on charges!"

Todd backed up, and the four companions instinctively clasped each other's hands for one brief moment. In that instant the Colonel seemed to get dizzy for a second and then he said, "I don't feel so well."

Jamal quipped, "Maybe you'd better go somewhere and lay down, man, cause you don't look too good."

"I think you're right, anyway... well done... well done. You're all to be congratulated on a job well done," he said while holding his head in his hands.

He was helped into a jeep by one of his soldiers and driven away into the night.

The intrepid band of warriors had a good laugh before turning and heading back to the command trailer where each one of them was able to make a call to their respective love ones to insure them that all was well.

Once back in the town of Acadia, they sat down to a hot meal of spaghetti and meatballs with broccoli and cheese and toasted garlic bread. Jamal being a vegetarian skipped the meatballs. Psych, Just kidding.

Jim was the first to speak, when they had finished eating.

"I'm not going to pretend that I understand what went on back there at the plant, but I think that, individually, each one of us must possess some kind of psychic ability. For example, Jennifer, Jamal, and myself have these precognitive dreams."

"But what about me?" Todd interjected. "I don't seem to have any sort of psychic ability or talent."

"Oh, but you do!" Jim exclaimed.

"You're the most gifted one of us all. That would explain why you were able to be there whenever something bad was about to happen. And don't forget it was you all along, that thing we know as Franz Zimmerman was trying to kill."

Jennifer shouted, "Oh, my God."

"What is it?" Todd asked alarmed.

"Now I know it was Todd who kept that thing from seeing me when I was dreaming about it. I used to think it was Jim who was helping me, but now I know it was Todd."

"Yes," said Jim, "that would be about right. You are the glue that has bonded us together Todd, and together we have what we can only be described as a terrible power. But we must only use it in this capacity for the forces of good." Then with a smile Jim said, "And I have a plan to ensure exactly that."

The Finger Lake Nuclear Plant had received only minimal structural damage as a result the skirmish with Hansragoth, and was back on line within the month.

Ron Kerber was now the plant's named director due to his leadership during the time of crisis. But he would forever know it had been a close call. Almost too close.

CHAPTER 27

One month later, at a sumptuous villa in Negril Jamaica, a double wedding ceremony was performed on a golden sunlit day.

Todd Morrison and Brighty Morgan were married along with Jim Green and Beverly Stokes. Jamal Walker was the best man and his wife, Iris, along with Jennifer, were the bridesmaids.

There would be no honeymoons.

Todd, Brighty, Jim and Jamal had all quit their jobs, and Todd and Jamal had moved their families to Negril. Beverly and Jim arranged for apartments to be sectioned off in the huge villa. For everyone would be living there now, permanently.

With Beverly's huge fortune of nearly sixty million dollars at their disposal, they would never have to worry about anything for the rest of their lives, but after the wedding their true work would begin.

In every room of the villa there was a brand new shortwave radio.

No one was really sure if the advent of Hansrogoth was the harbinger of worse things to come, but Jim felt they would have to be prepared and keep their ears open to the rest of the world, as a blind gentleman named Ray Williams had done so many, many months before, for any event or occurrence that might point in that dark direction.

The wedding was a huge success, and in the following weeks afterwards, everyone settled down into a routine of exercise and leisure as well as tutoring for the kids.

Then one day, Todd was sitting on the beach listening to his portable short wave radio when he heard a broadcast that turned his face grim and his heart cold. He immediately got up and walked back to the villa by the pool, where everyone else had just started to have lunch.

He walked slowly as if he carried the weight of the world upon his shoulders and his shoulders alone.

As he approached, the look on his face spread fear and alarm through his companions.

With deep sadness in his voice he said, "Jim, Jamal, Jennifer, I think you'd all better listen to this."

He sat the radio down on the table and turned up the volume as the shortwave broadcast he had first heard on the beach began to repeat itself over and over again.

It would continue to repeat itself to a world that would soon grow dark and cold while panic and despair reigned supreme.

As for Jim, Todd, Jennifer and Jamal they understood that they now faced a battle many times greater than the one they had fought against Hansragoth. And the battle had just begun.

Fore on the shortwave a faint but deep brooding voice could be heard saying:

"Prepare thyself for the Master cometh."

"Prepare thyself for the Master cometh."
"Prepare thyself for the Master cometh."
"Prepare thyself... "

ABOUT THE AUTHOR

Dexter Wansel is a resident of Philadelphia, Pa. Although, he and his wife Judith spend much of their time in Lewes, Delaware with his parents Phyllis and Corel. Dexter has garnered much success as a producer/arranger/composer whose works can be heard throughout the Pop/R+B catalogs. From Lou Rawls and Patti Labelle to Jay-z and Trey Songz as well as works of his own. He has won numerous awards and has many gold and platinum albums to his credit. His last music CD "Digital Groove World" can be found at many store kiosks and online. Dexter is currently working on a sequel to this novel, as well as producing and writing arrangements for some of today's hottest recording artists.